Roller-Coaster Grandma

By
Dr. Ruth K. Westheimer
and Pierre A. Lehu

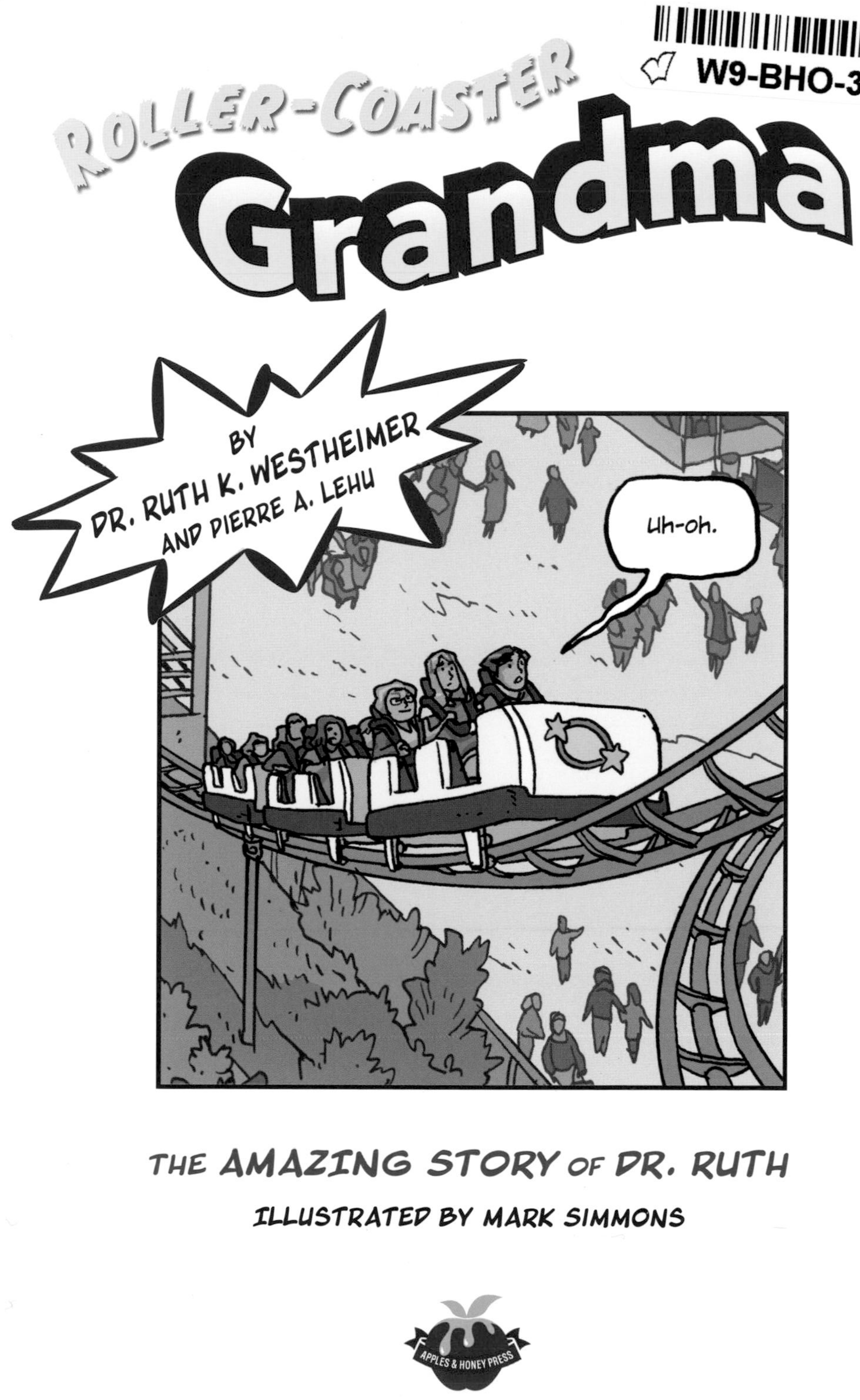
Uh-oh.

The Amazing Story of Dr. Ruth

Illustrated by Mark Simmons

Apples & Honey Press

For my four grandchildren, Ari, Leora, Michal, and Ben, who were the inspiration for this book and who inspire me every day with their talents, family values, and love for their Omi.
– R.K.W.

For my three grandchildren, Jude, Rhys, and Isabelle.
– P.L.

For Rich and Rhoda, Bill and Bev, and Julie most of all.
– M.S.

If I teach you something by which you shall live, will you learn it?
—Talmud *Sanhedrin*

The song that Karola sings on the train is excerpted from the song "Jeder Mensch auf der Welt." It begins:

Every person in the world
Has his own country
And there he is at home
Only one people in the world has no homeland of their own
And every day there stands before them
The eternal Jewish question,
Whither Jew?
Who in the world will take you?
Where can you be safe?

The flashbacks in this book are all based on real events.
The amusement park story is fictional.

Apples & Honey Press
An imprint of Behrman House
Millburn, NJ 07041

www.applesandhoneypress.com

Text copyright © 2018 by Dr. Ruth K. Westheimer and Pierre A. Lehu
Illustrations copyright ©2018 by Apples and Honey Press
All photographs are courtesy of Ruth K. Westheimer.

ISBN 978-1-68115-532-6

Cover design by Elynn Cohen
Edited by Ann D. Koffsky
Printed in China

1 3 5 7 9 8 6 4 2

Library of Congress Cataloging-in-Publication Data

Names: Westheimer, Ruth K. (Ruth Karola), 1928- author. I Lehu, Pierre A., author. I Simmons, Marc, illustrator.
Title: Rollercoaster grandma! : the true story of Dr. Ruth / by Dr. Ruth K. Westheimer and Pierre A. Lehu; illustrated by Marc Simmons.

Description: Springfield, NJ : Apples & Honey Press, [2017] I Summary: While visiting an amusement park with her grandchildren, Dr. Ruth Westheimer relates tales from her childhood in Nazi Germany, through her becoming a famous radio and television personality in the United States.

Identifiers: LCCN 2017000731 I ISBN 9781681155326
Subjects: LCSH: Westheimer, Ruth K. (Ruth Karola), 1928—Juvenile fiction. I Graphic novels. I CYAC: Westheimer, Ruth K. (Ruth Karola), 1928—Fiction. I Graphic novels. I Psychologists—Fiction. I Jews—United States—Fiction. I Grandmothers—Fiction. I Amusement parks—Fiction.Classification: LCC PZ7.7.W477 Rol 2017 I DDC 741.5/31—dc23 LC record available at https://lccn.loc.gov/2017000731

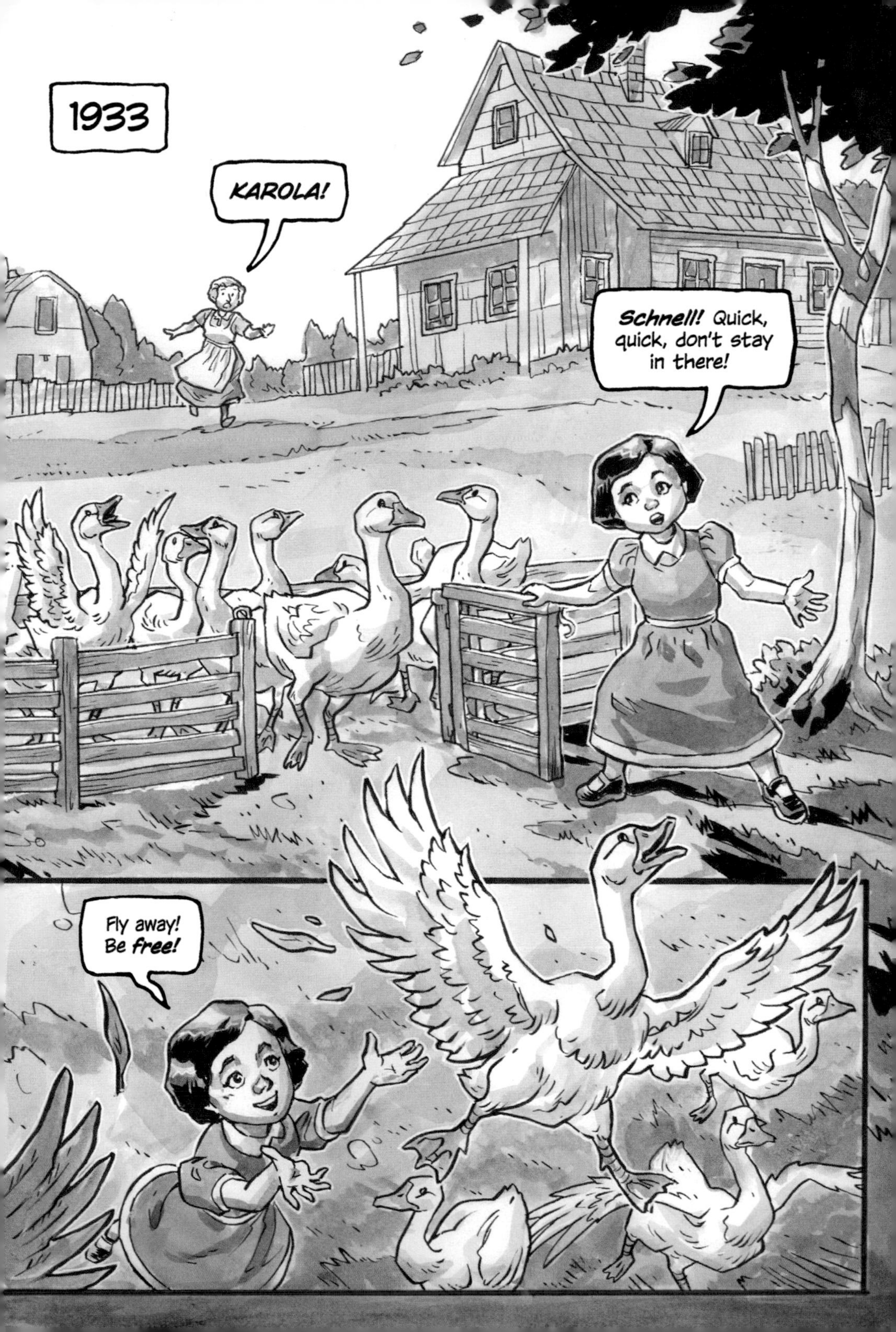
1933
KAROLA!
Schnell! Quick, quick, don't stay in there!
Fly away! Be free!

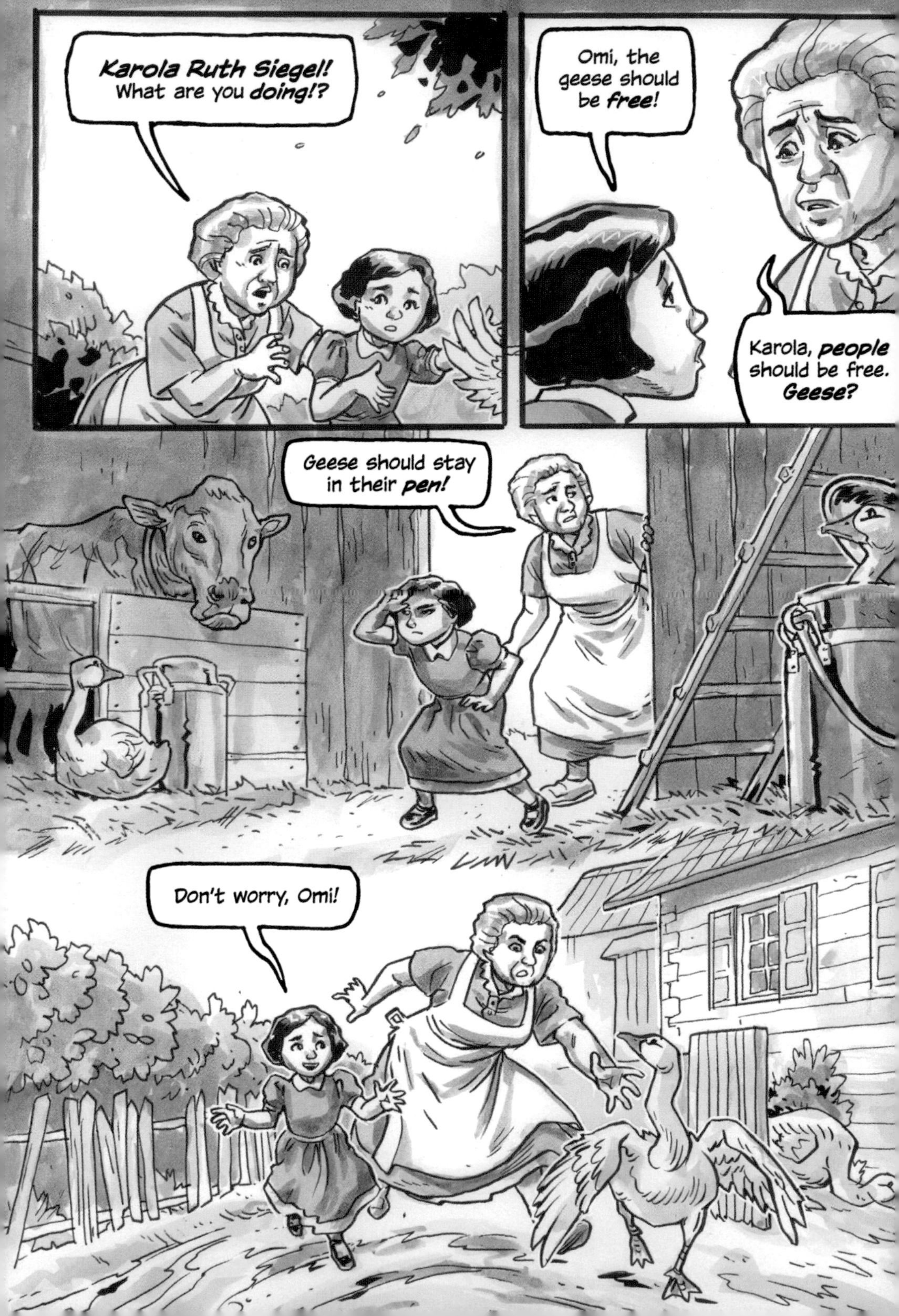
Karola Ruth Siegel! What are you doing!?
Omi, the geese should be free!
Karola, people should be free. Geese?
Geese should stay in their pen!
Don't worry, Omi!

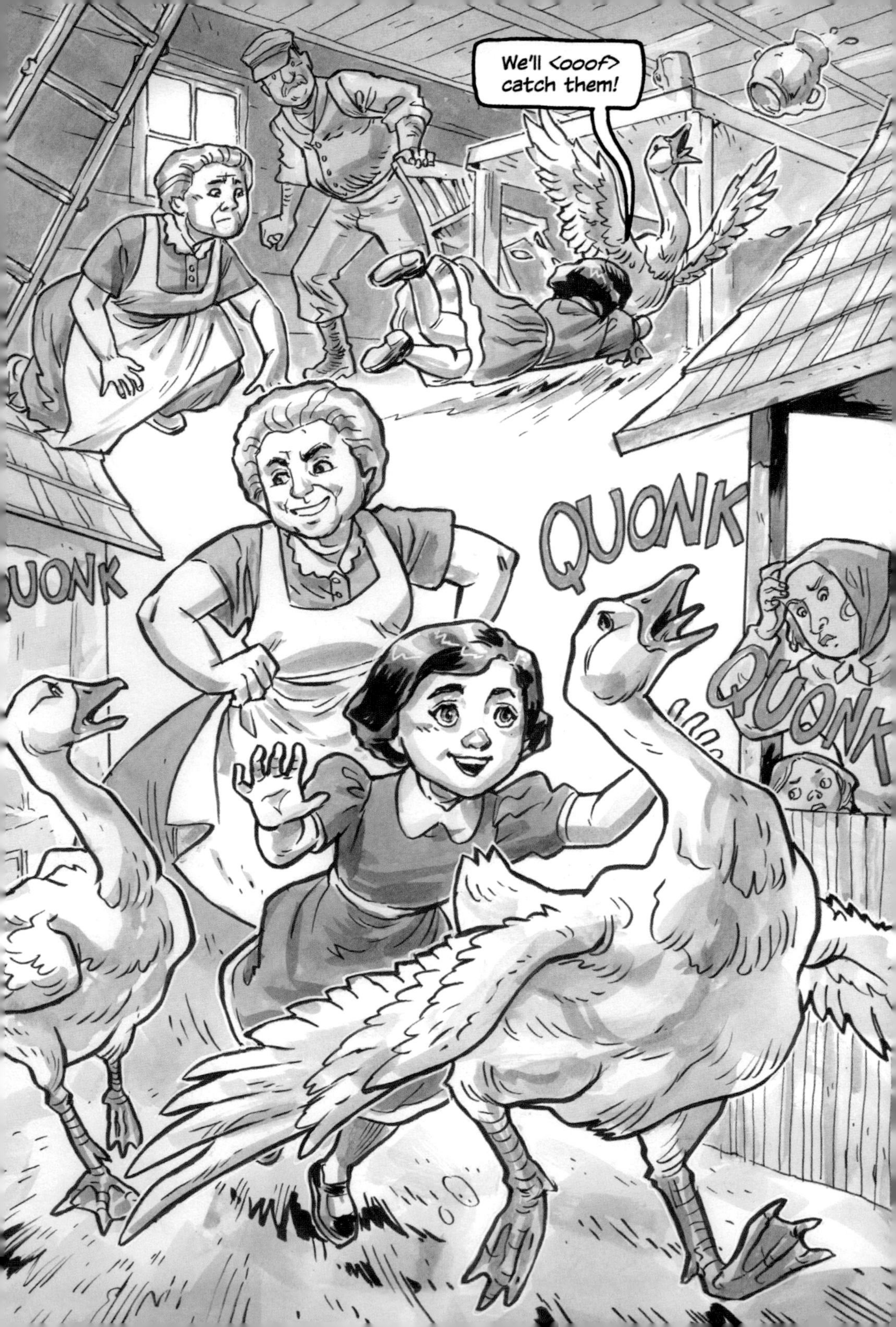
We'll <ooof> catch them!
QUONK
QUONK
QUONK

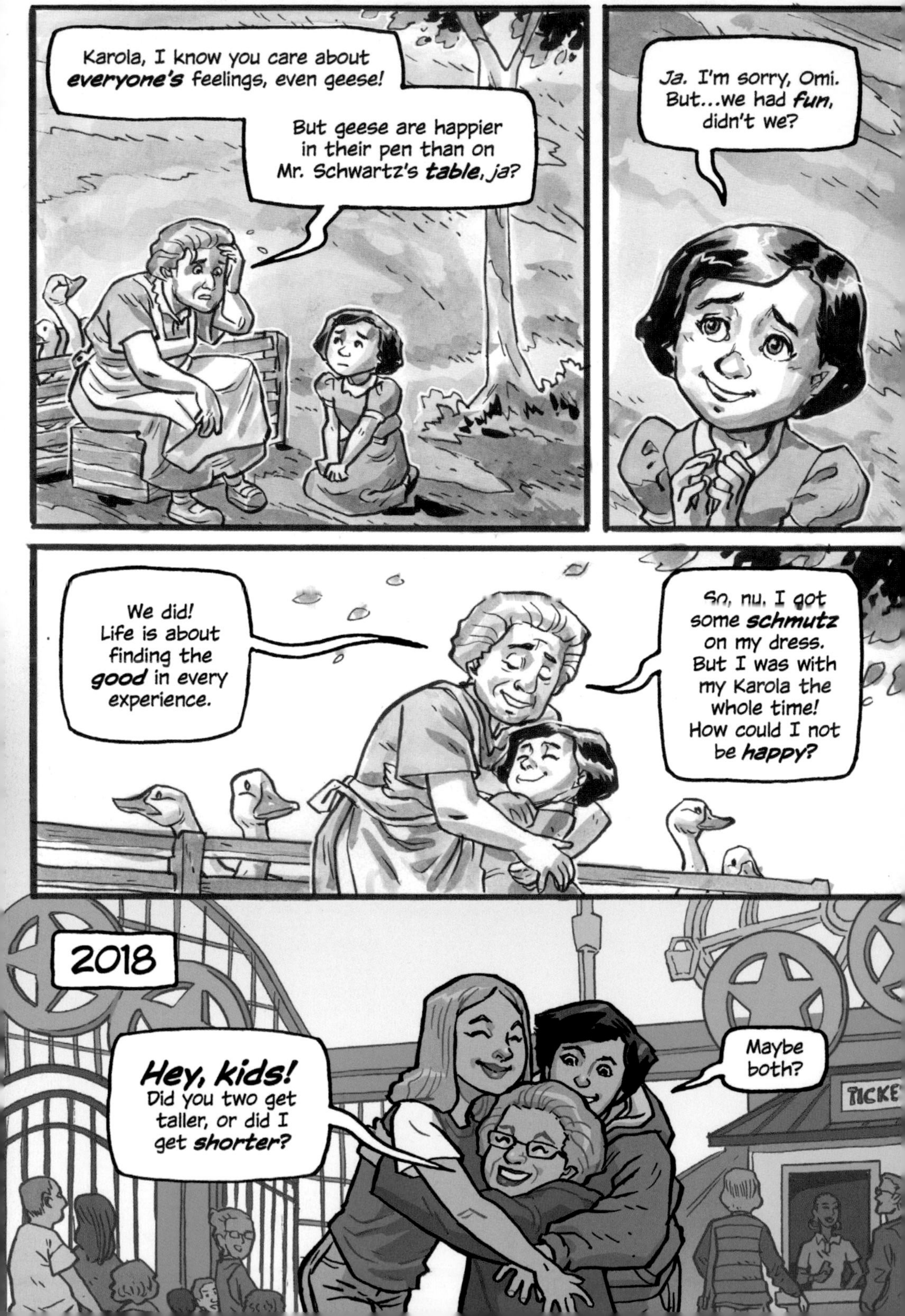
Karola, I know you care about ***everyone's*** feelings, even geese!
But geese are happier in their pen than on Mr. Schwartz's ***table***, *ja?*
Ja. I'm sorry, Omi. But...we had ***fun***, didn't we?
We did! Life is about finding the ***good*** in every experience.
So, nu. I got some ***schmutz*** on my dress. But I was with my Karola the whole time! How could I not be ***happy?***
2018
Hey, kids! Did you two get taller, or did I get ***shorter?***
Maybe both?
TICKE

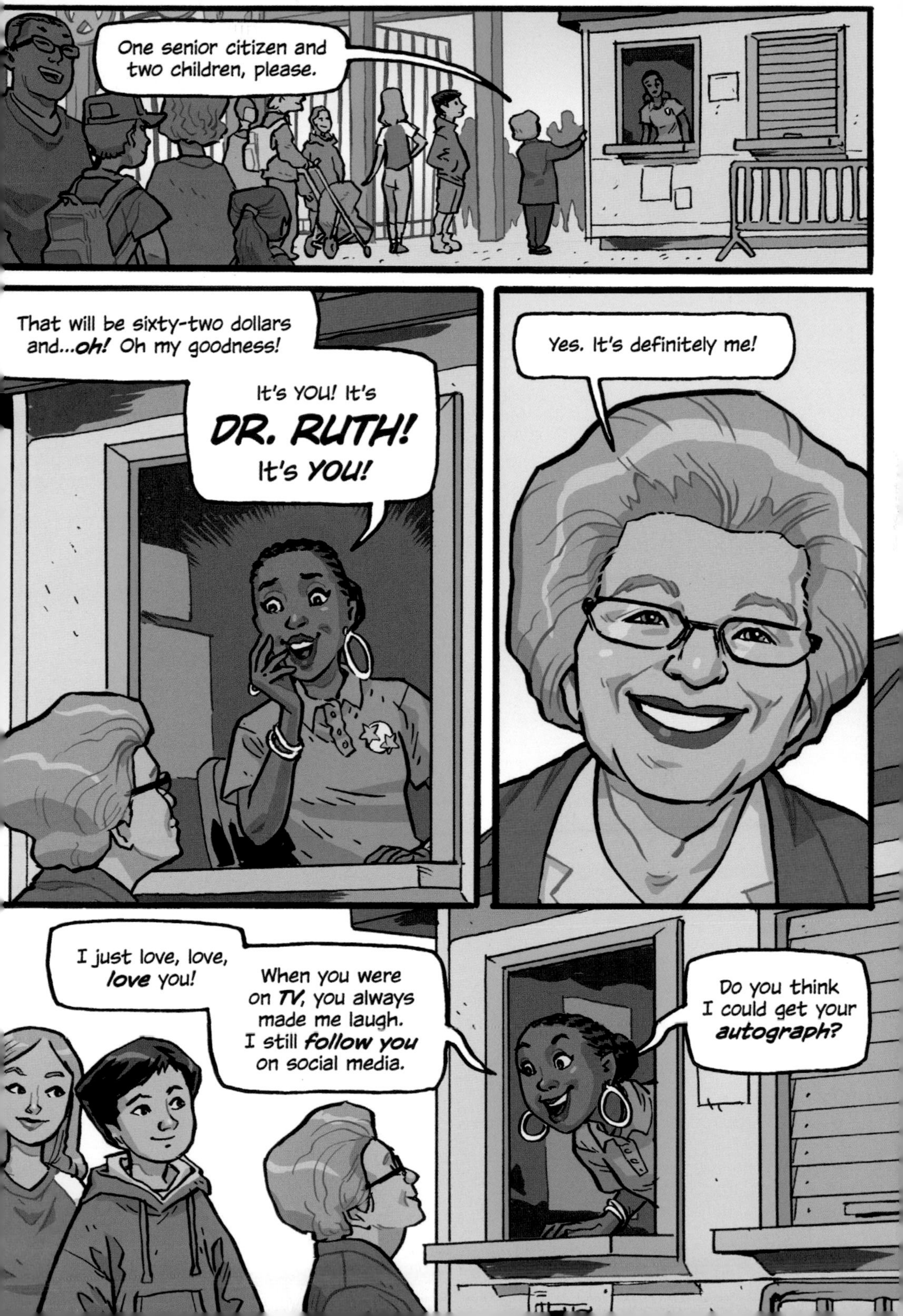

One senior citizen and two children, please.
That will be sixty-two dollars and...oh! Oh my goodness!
It's YOU! It's DR. RUTH! It's YOU!
Yes. It's definitely me!
I just love, love, love you!
When you were on TV, you always made me laugh. I still follow you on social media.
Do you think I could get your autograph?

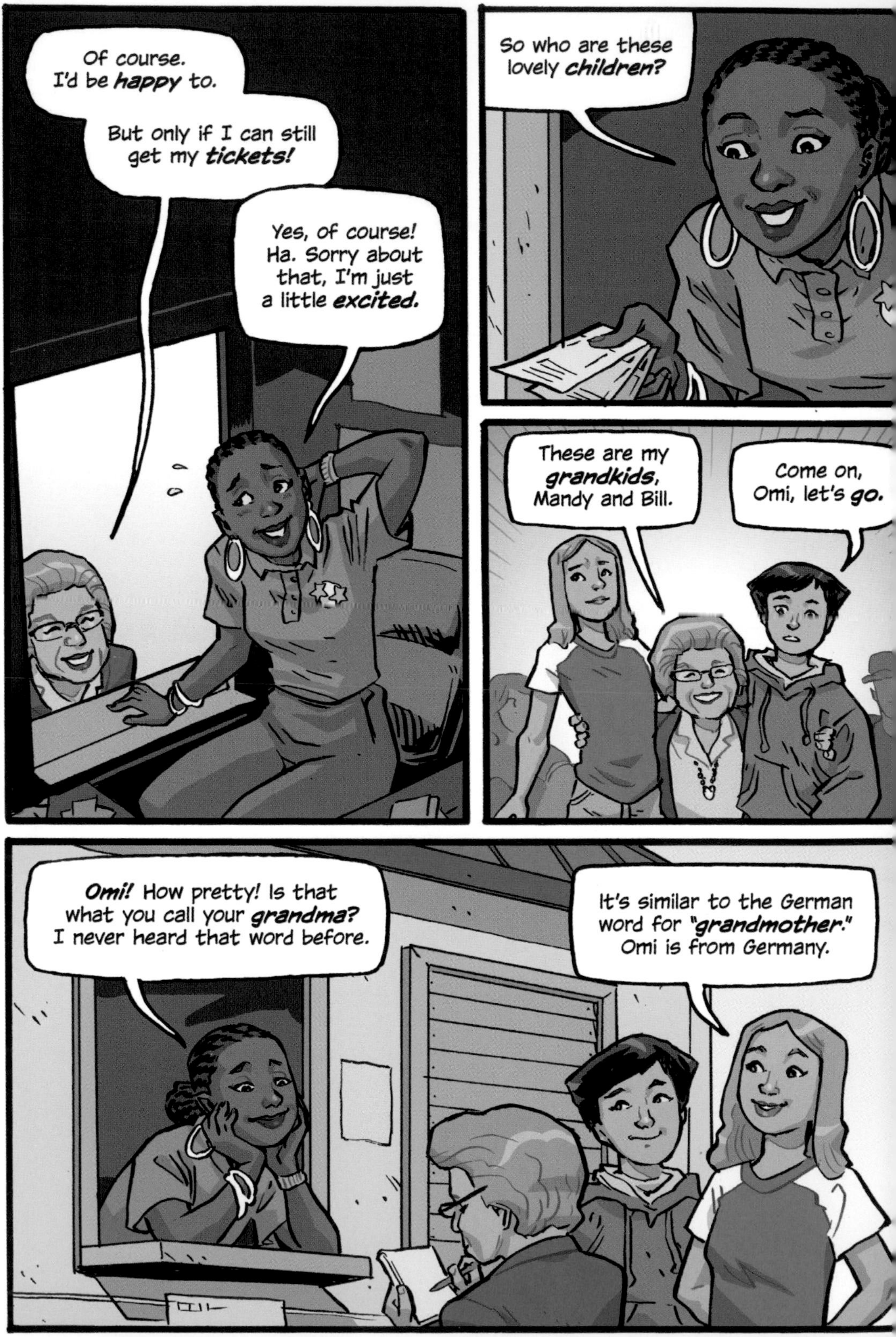
Of course. I'd be happy to.
But only if I can still get my tickets!
Yes, of course! Ha. Sorry about that, I'm just a little excited.
So who are these lovely children?
These are my grandkids, Mandy and Bill.
Come on, Omi, let's go.
Omi! How pretty! Is that what you call your grandma? I never heard that word before.
It's similar to the German word for "grandmother." Omi is from Germany.

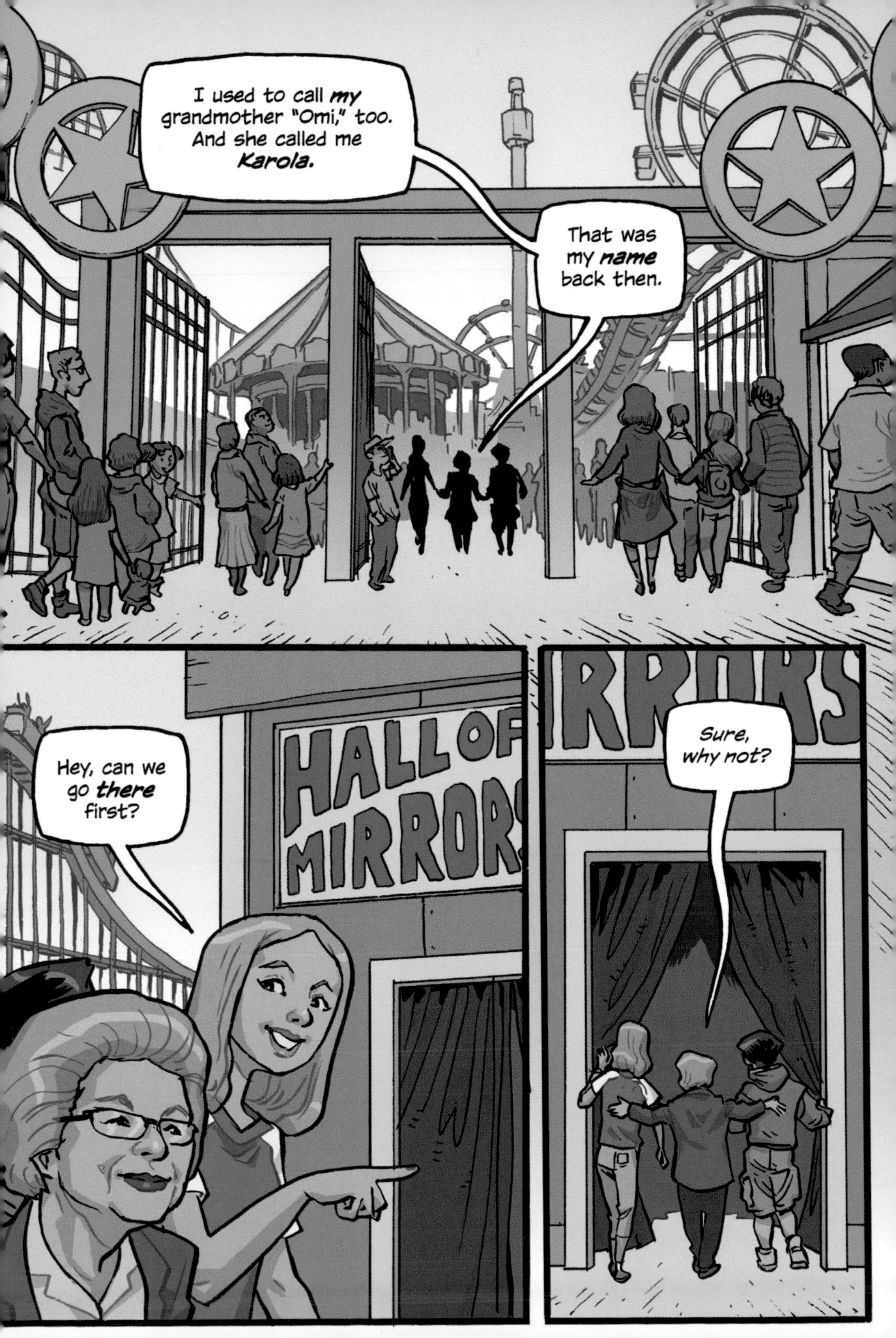
I used to call *my* grandmother "Omi," too. And she called me *Karola.*
That was my *name* back then.
HALL OF MIRRORS
Hey, can we go *there* first?
IRRORS
Sure, why not?

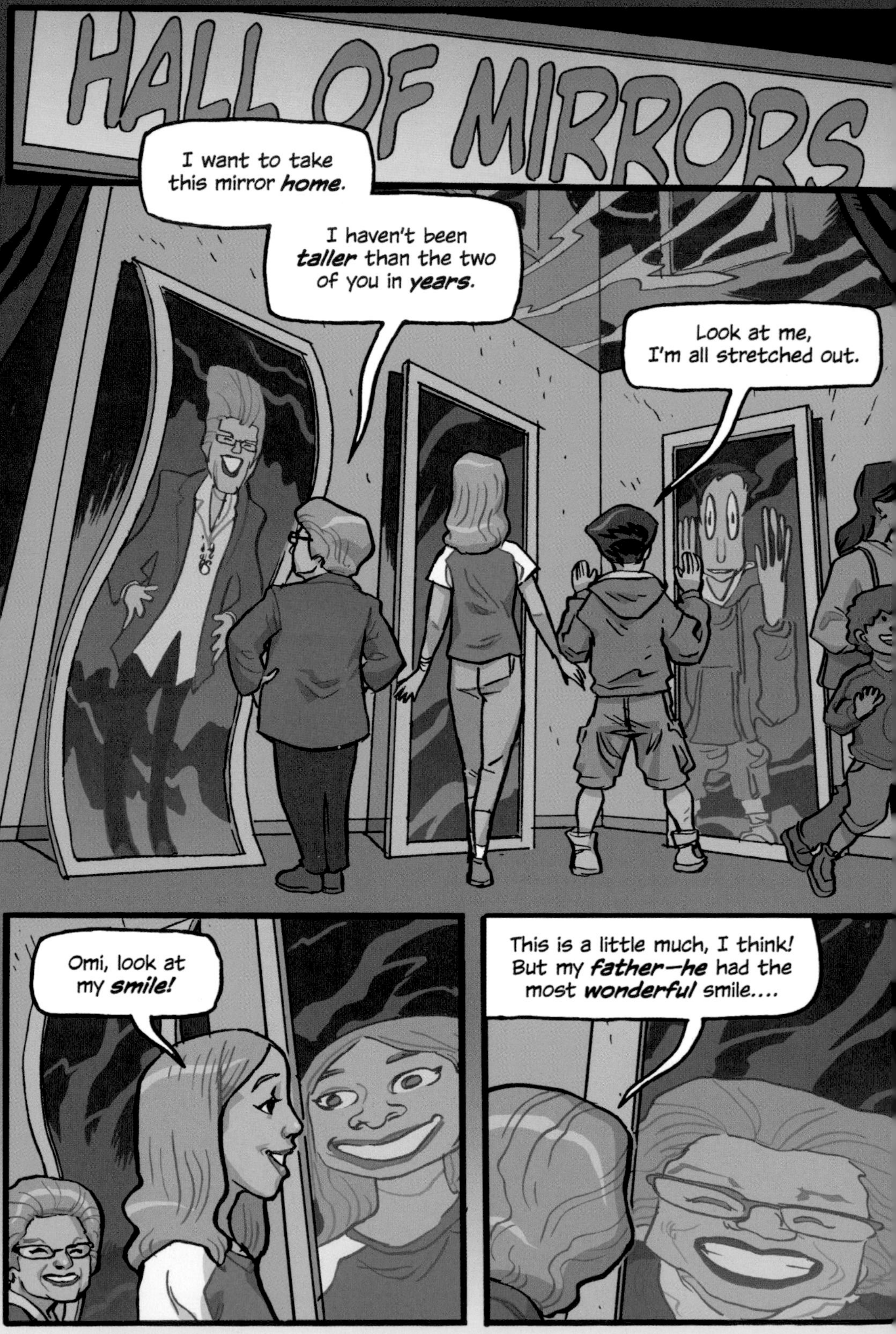
HALL OF MIRRORS
I want to take this mirror home.
I haven't been taller than the two of you in years.
Look at me, I'm all stretched out.
Omi, look at my smile!
This is a little much, I think! But my father—he had the most wonderful smile....

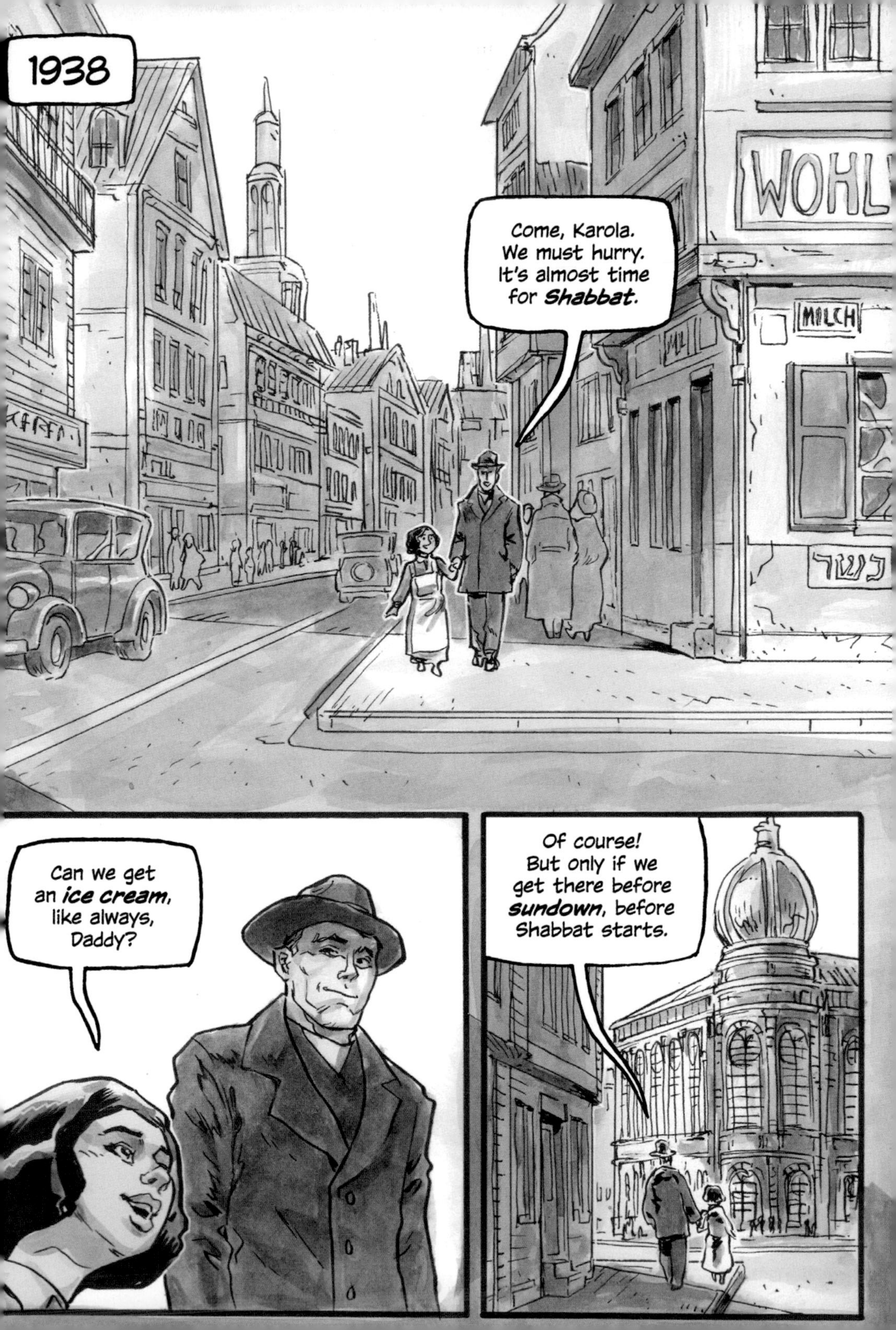
1938
WOHL
MILCH
Come, Karola. We must hurry. It's almost time for ***Shabbat***.
Can we get an ***ice cream***, like always, Daddy?
Of course! But only if we get there before ***sundown***, before Shabbat starts.

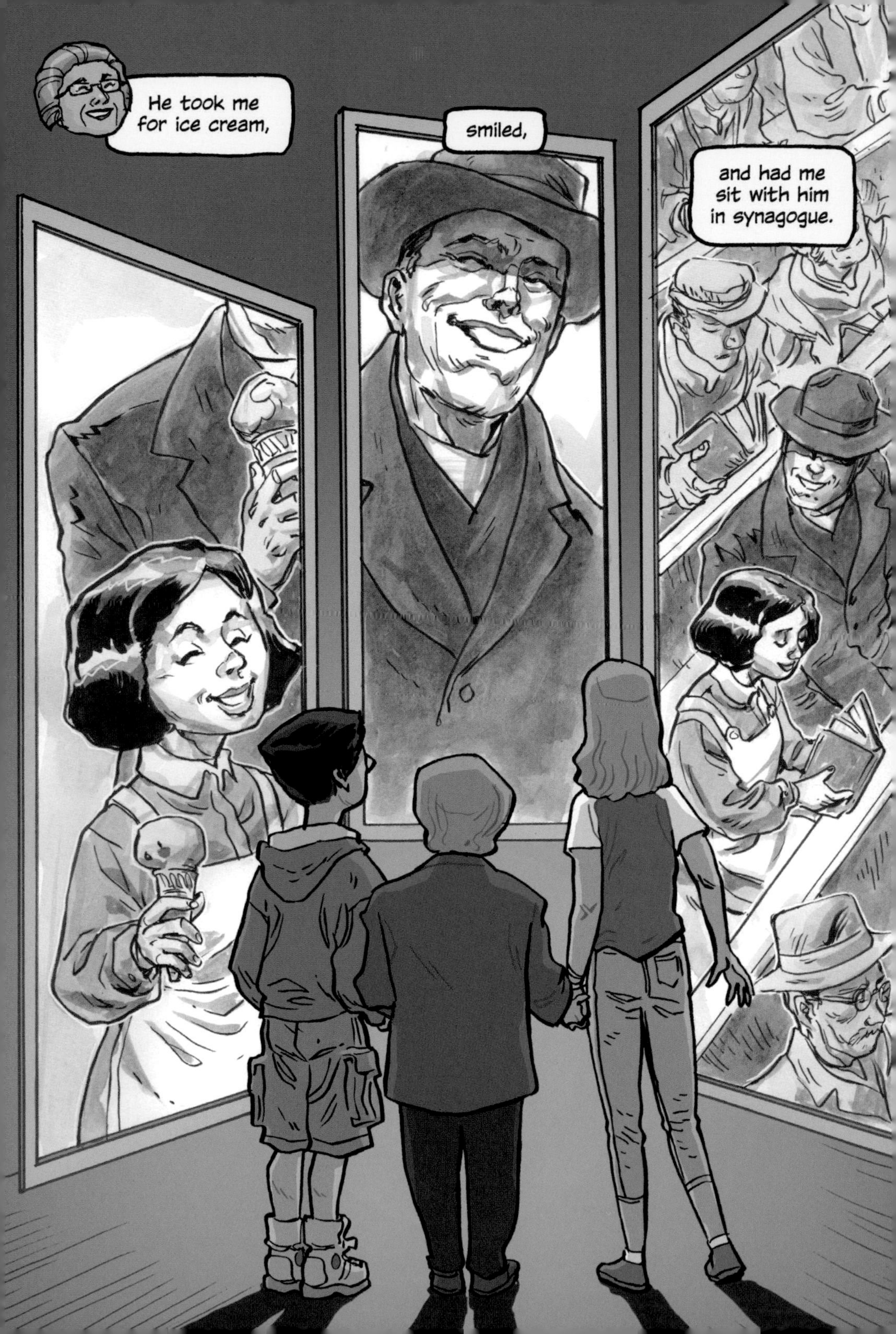
He took me for ice cream,
smiled,
and had me sit with him in synagogue.

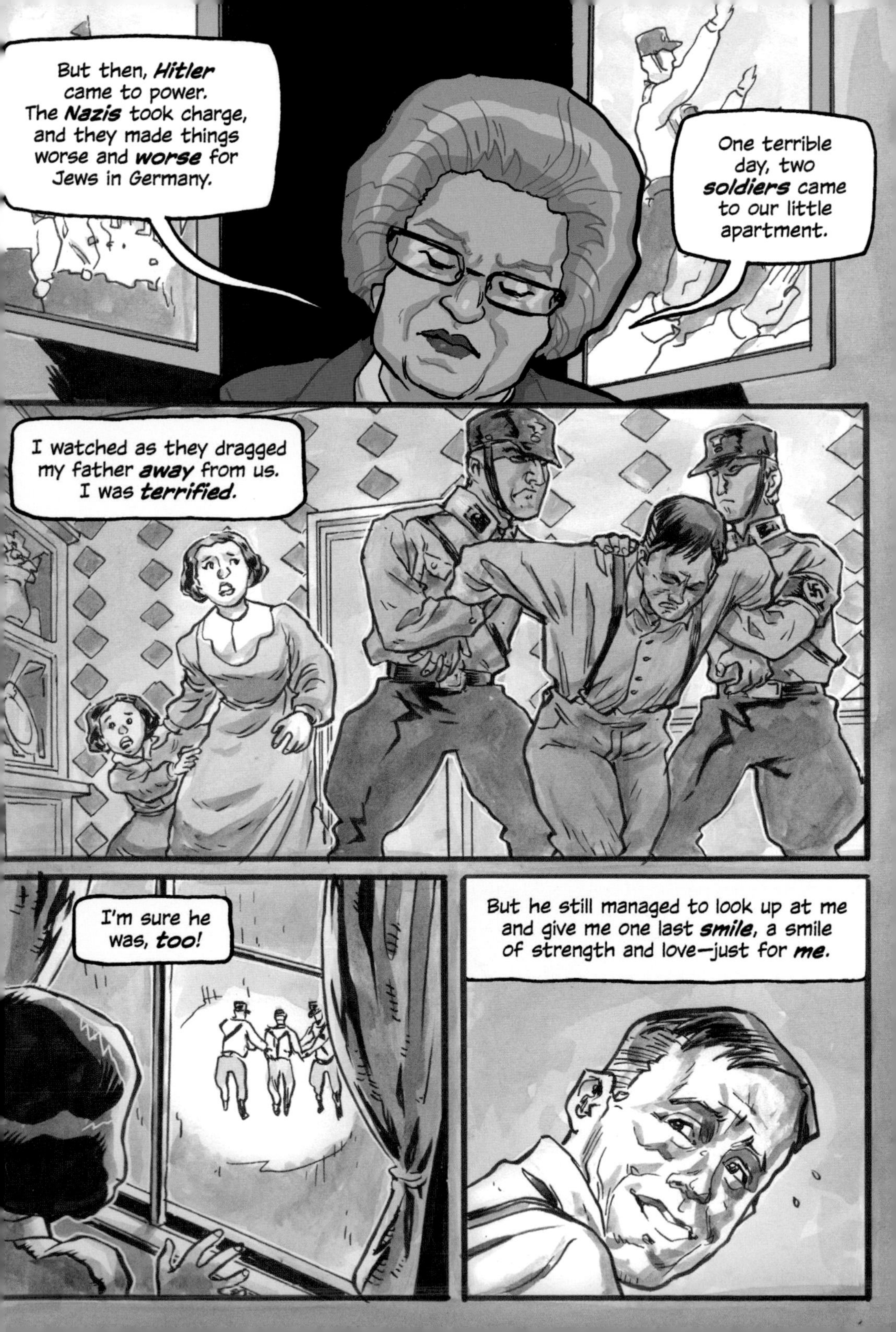

But then, *Hitler* came to power. The *Nazis* took charge, and they made things worse and *worse* for Jews in Germany.
One terrible day, two *soldiers* came to our little apartment.
I watched as they dragged my father *away* from us. I was *terrified*.
I'm sure he was, *too*!
But he still managed to look up at me and give me one last *smile*, a smile of strength and love—just for *me*.

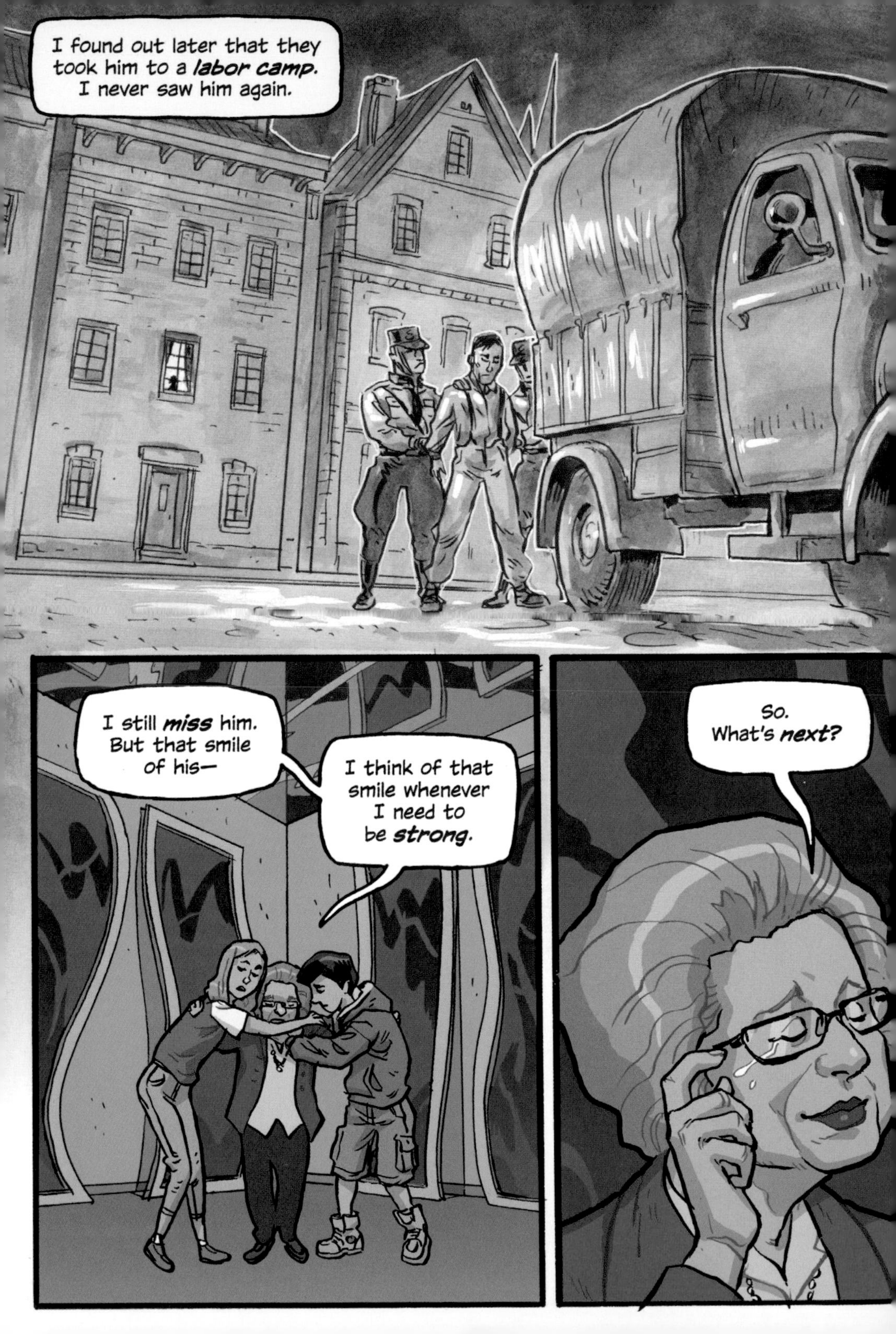
I found out later that they took him to a *labor camp*. I never saw him again.
I still *miss* him. But that smile of his—
I think of that smile whenever I need to be *strong*.
So. What's *next?*

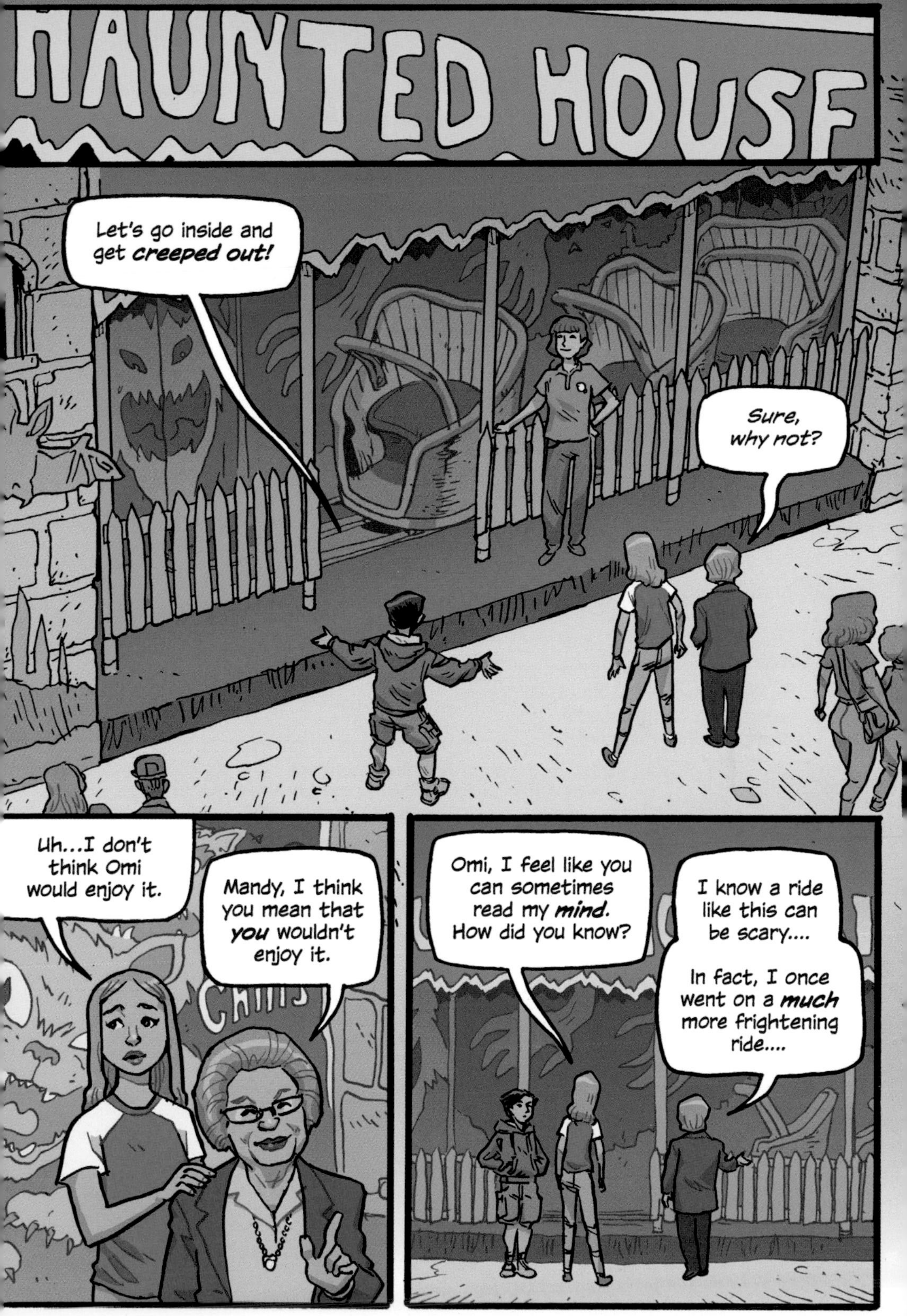
HAUNTED HOUSE
Let's go inside and get ***creeped out!***
Sure, why not?
Uh...I don't think Omi would enjoy it.
Mandy, I think you mean that ***you*** wouldn't enjoy it.
Omi, I feel like you can sometimes read my ***mind***. How did you know?
I know a ride like this can be scary....
In fact, I once went on a ***much*** more frightening ride....

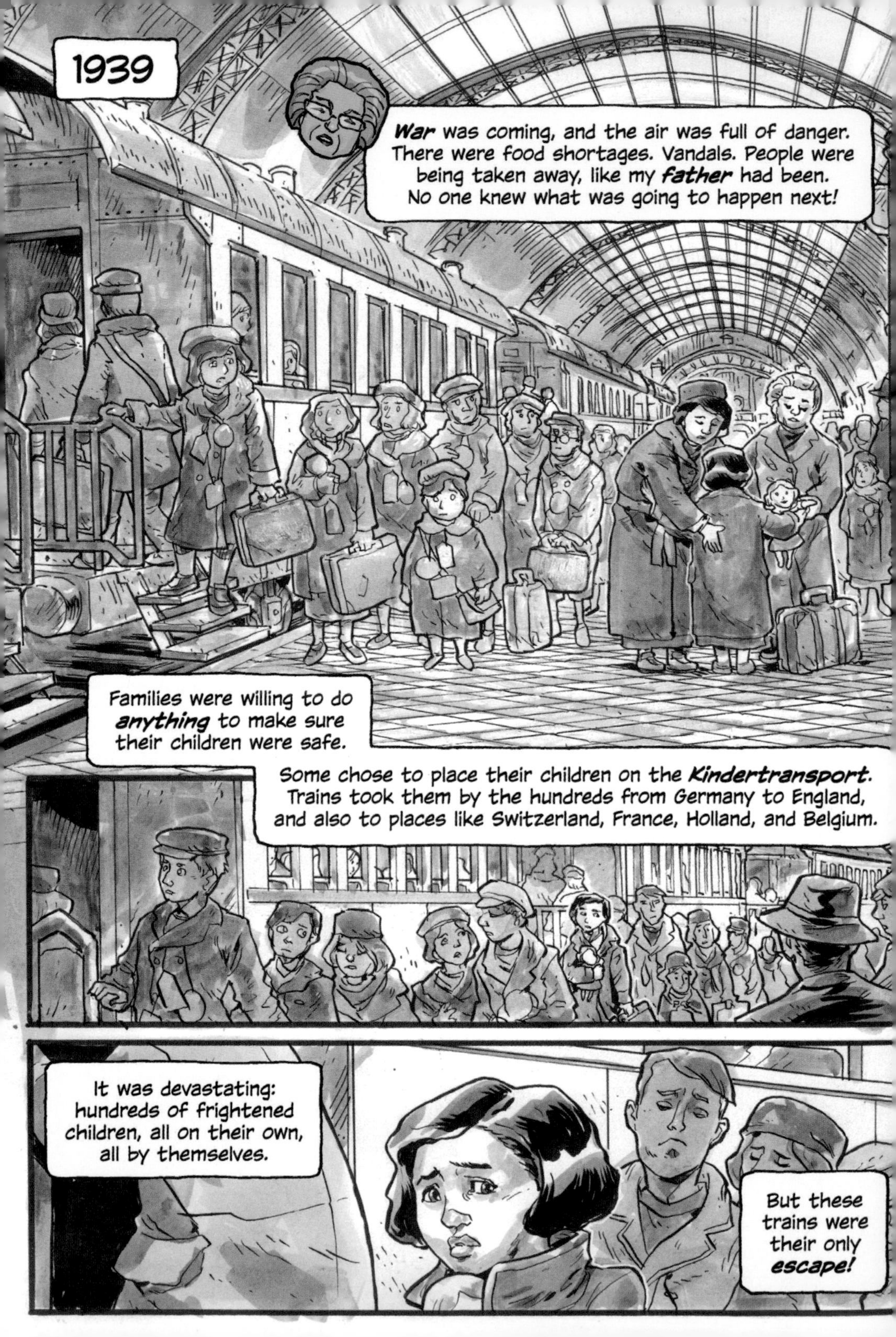
1939
War was coming, and the air was full of danger. There were food shortages. Vandals. People were being taken away, like my father had been. No one knew what was going to happen next!
Families were willing to do anything to make sure their children were safe.
Some chose to place their children on the Kindertransport. Trains took them by the hundreds from Germany to England, and also to places like Switzerland, France, Holland, and Belgium.
It was devastating: hundreds of frightened children, all on their own, all by themselves.
But these trains were their only escape!

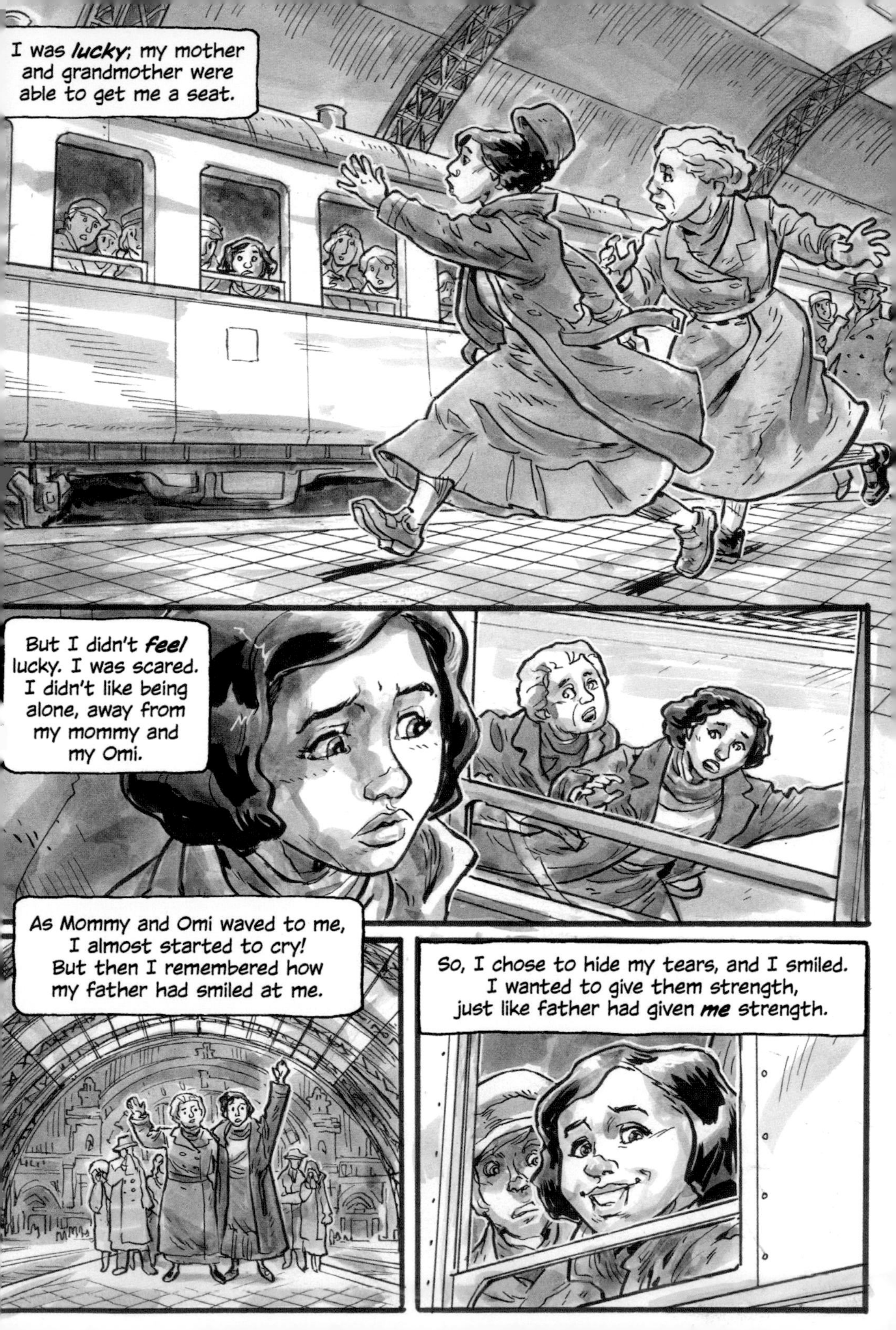

I was lucky; my mother and grandmother were able to get me a seat.
But I didn't feel lucky. I was scared. I didn't like being alone, away from my mommy and my Omi.
As Mommy and Omi waved to me, I almost started to cry! But then I remembered how my father had smiled at me.
So, I chose to hide my tears, and I smiled. I wanted to give them strength, just like father had given me strength.

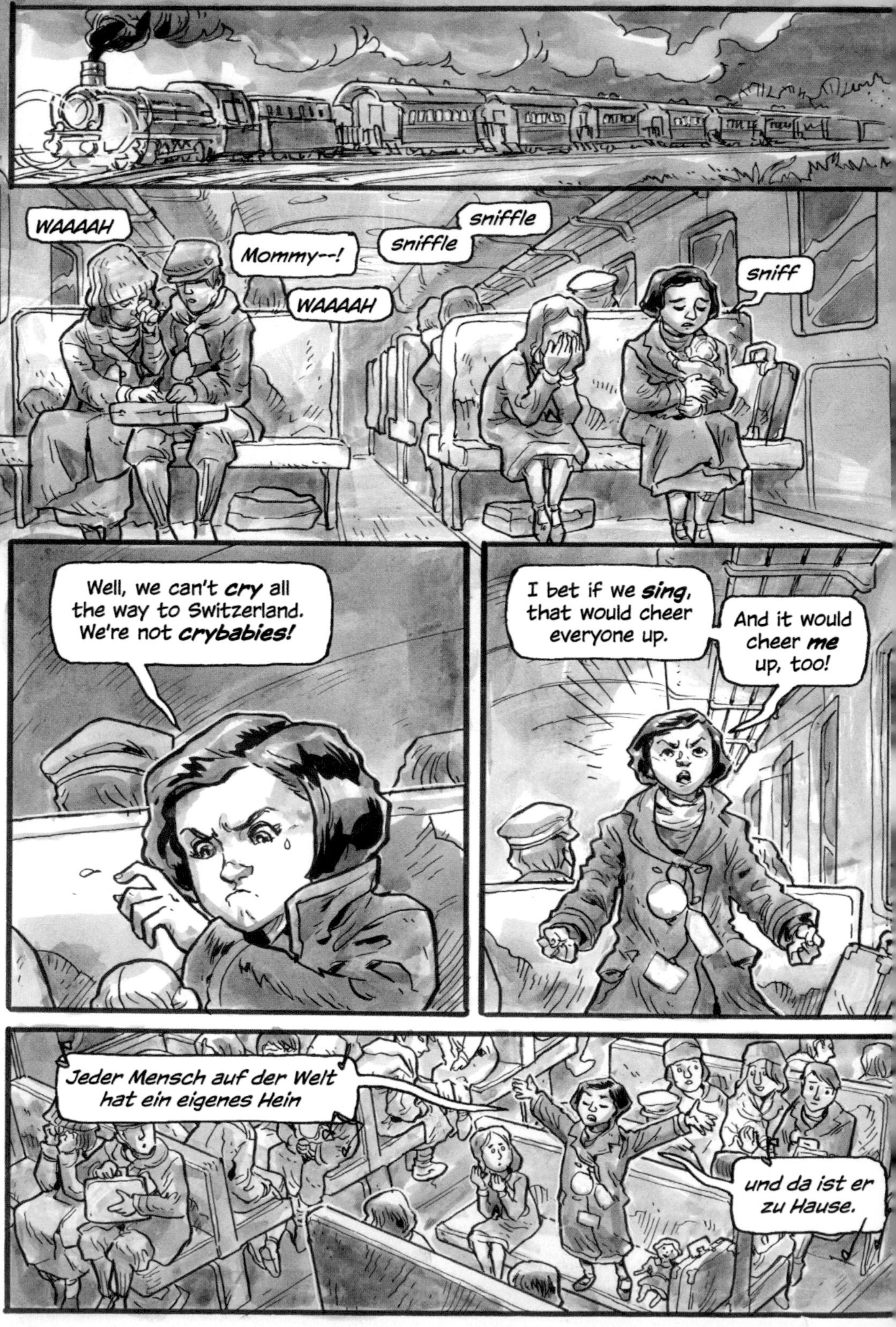
WAAAAH
Mommy--!
sniffle
sniffle
WAAAAH
sniff
Well, we can't cry all the way to Switzerland. We're not crybabies!
I bet if we sing, that would cheer everyone up.
And it would cheer me up, too!
Jeder Mensch auf der Welt hat ein eigenes Hein
und da ist er zu Hause.

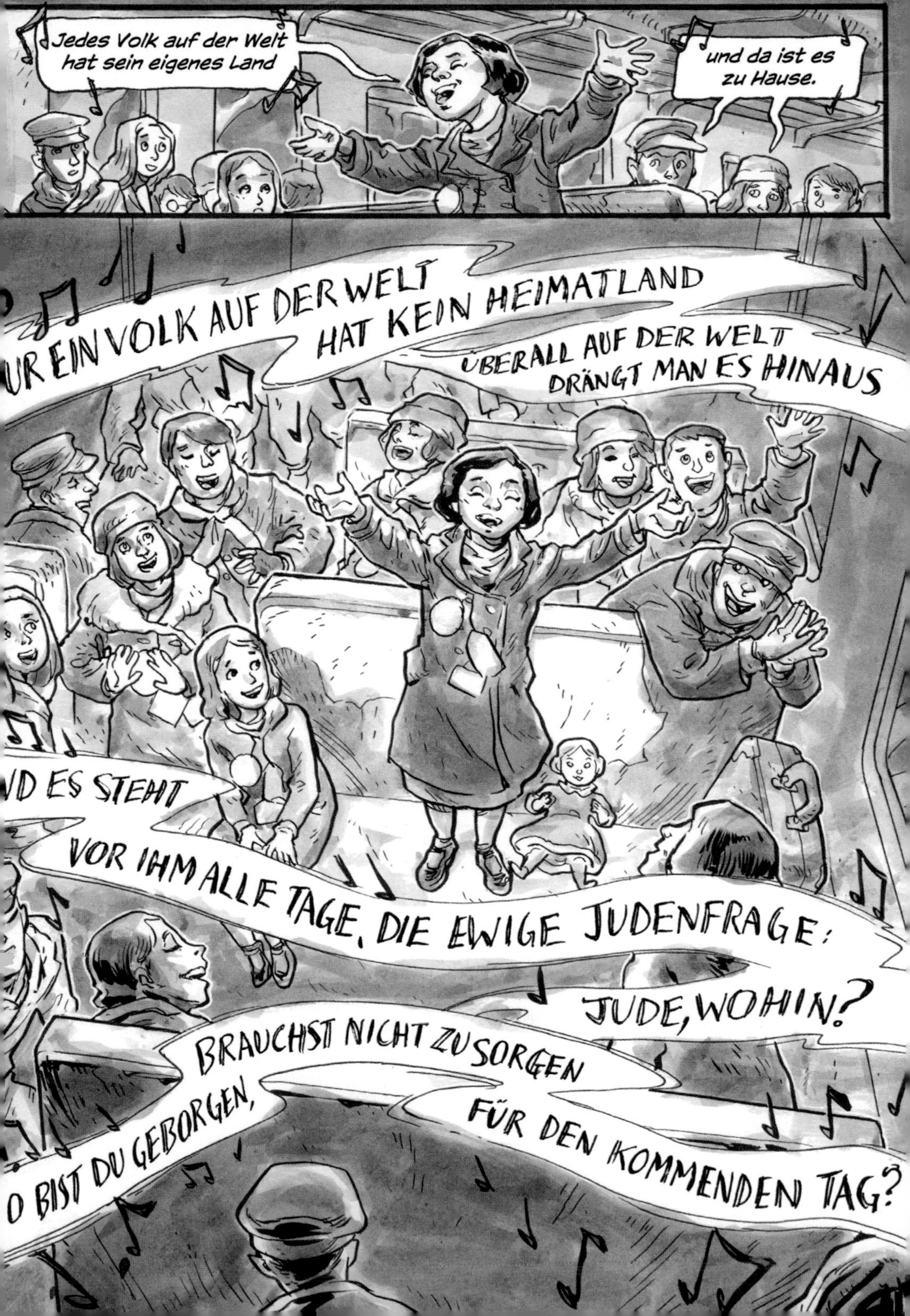
Jedes Volk auf der Welt hat sein eigenes Land
und da ist es zu Hause.
UR EIN VOLK AUF DER WELT HAT KEIN HEIMATLAND
ÜBERALL AUF DER WELT DRÄNGT MAN ES HINAUS
ND ES STEHT VOR IHM ALLE TAGE, DIE EWIGE JUDENFRAGE:
JUDE, WOHIN?
O BIST DU GEBORGEN,
BRAUCHST NICHT ZU SORGEN FÜR DEN KOMMENDEN TAG?

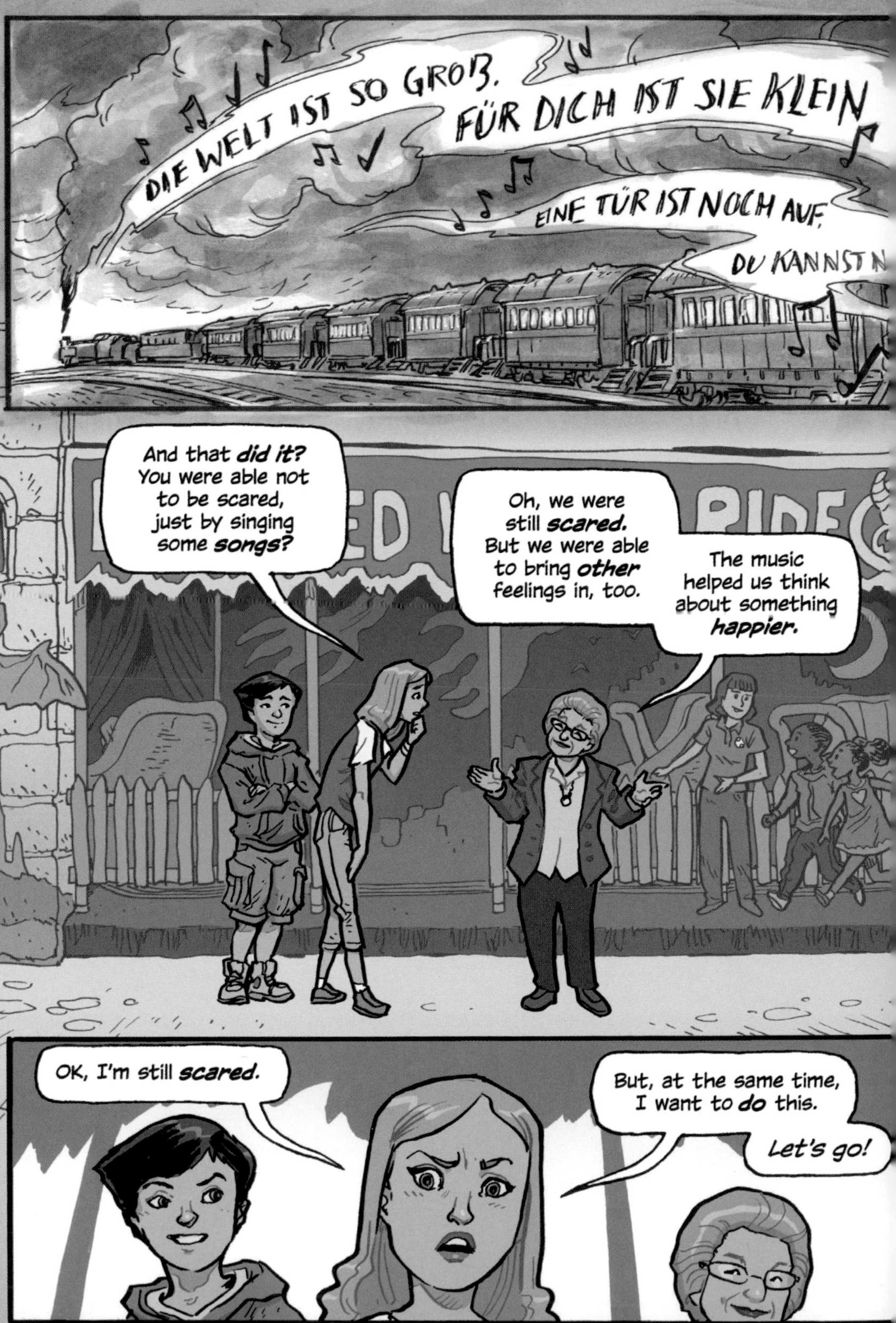

DIE WELT IST SO GROß.
FÜR DICH IST SIE KLEIN
EINE TÜR IST NOCH AUF,
DU KANNST N
And that *did it?* You were able not to be scared, just by singing some *songs?*
Oh, we were still *scared.* But we were able to bring *other* feelings in, too.
The music helped us think about something *happier.*
OK, I'm still *scared.*
But, at the same time, I want to *do* this.
Let's go!

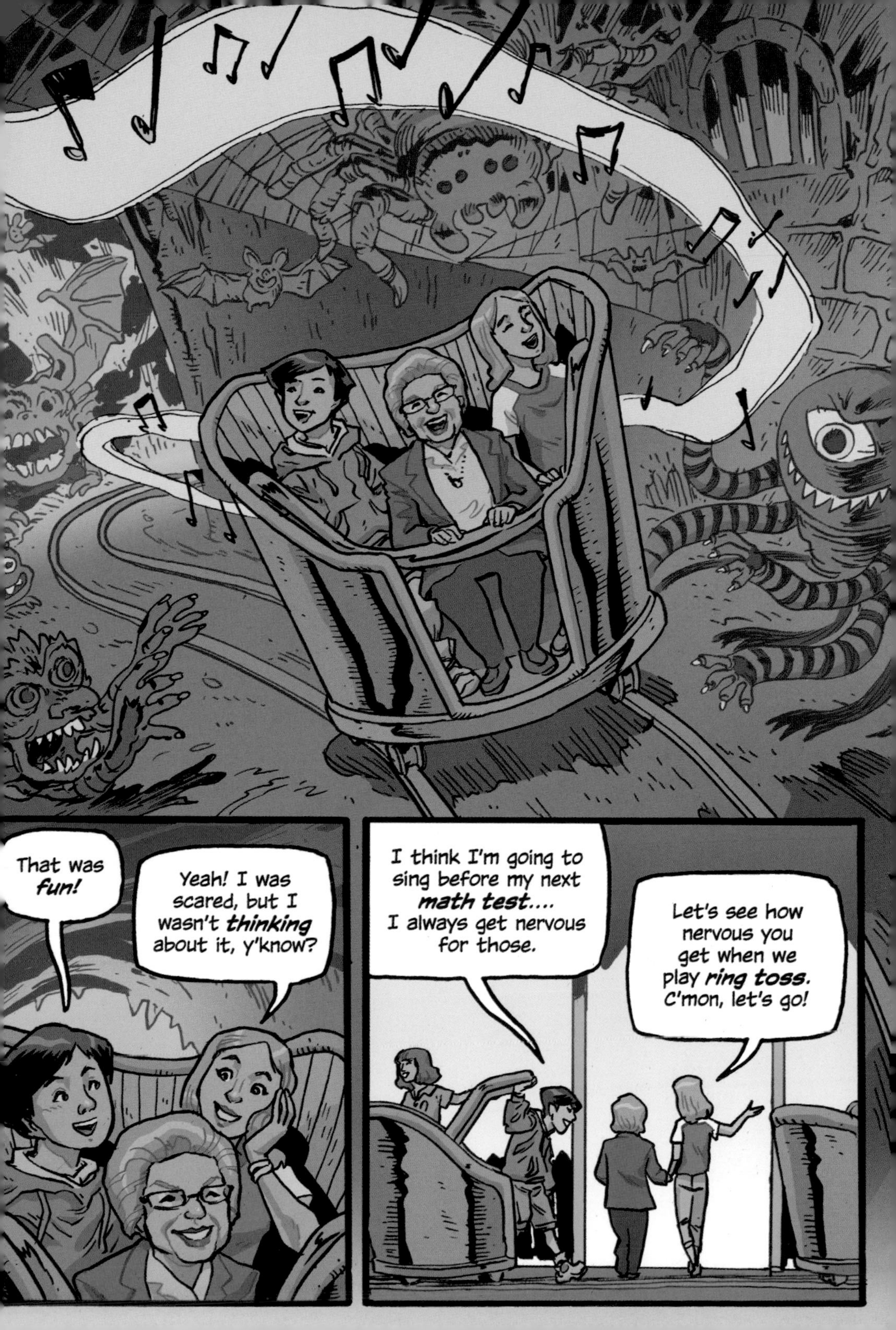
That was *fun!*
Yeah! I was scared, but I wasn't *thinking* about it, y'know?
I think I'm going to sing before my next *math test*.... I always get nervous for those.
Let's see how nervous you get when we play *ring toss*. C'mon, let's go!

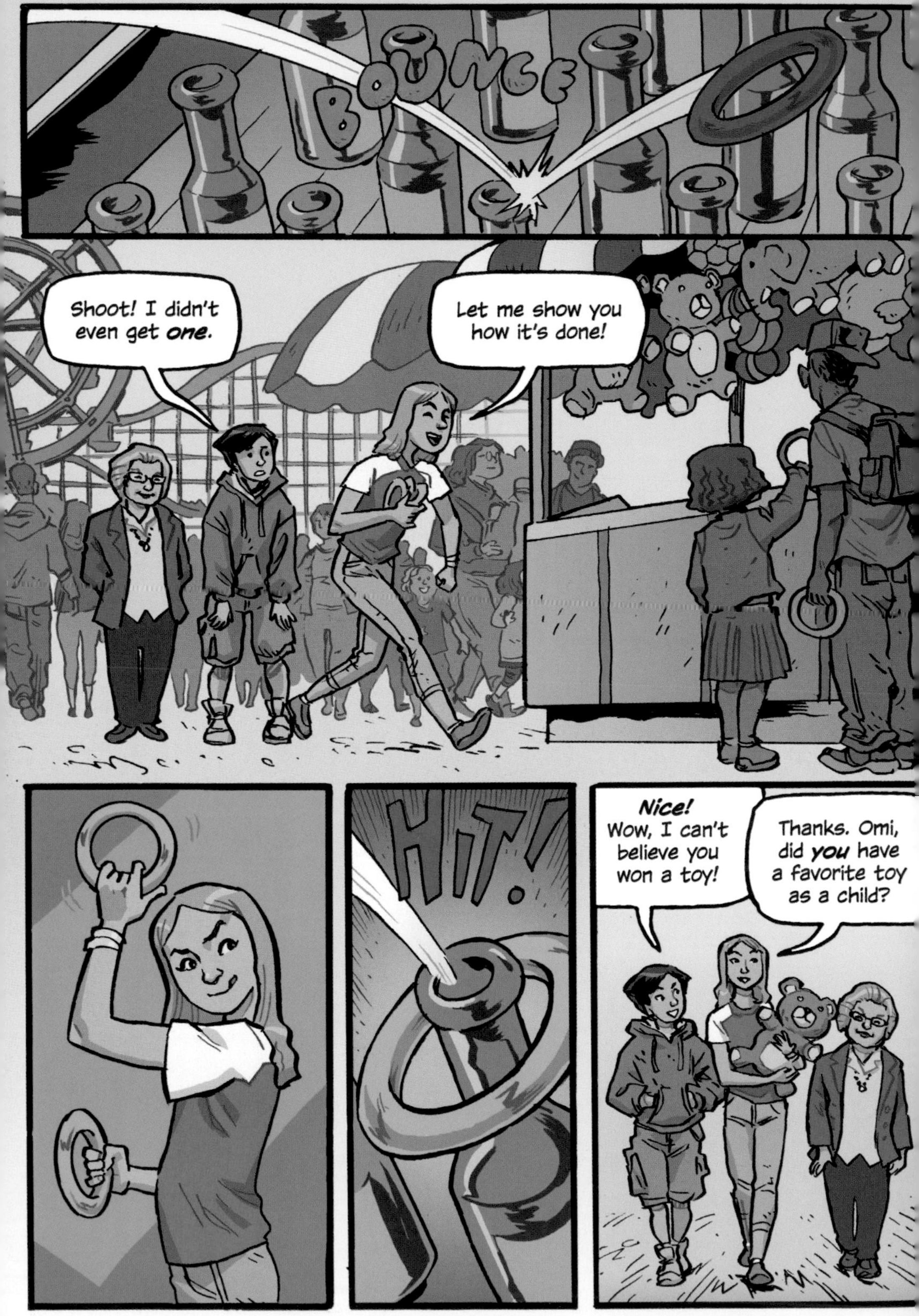
BOUNCE
Shoot! I didn't even get *one*.
Let me show you how it's done!
HIT!
Nice! Wow, I can't believe you won a toy!
Thanks. Omi, did *you* have a favorite toy as a child?

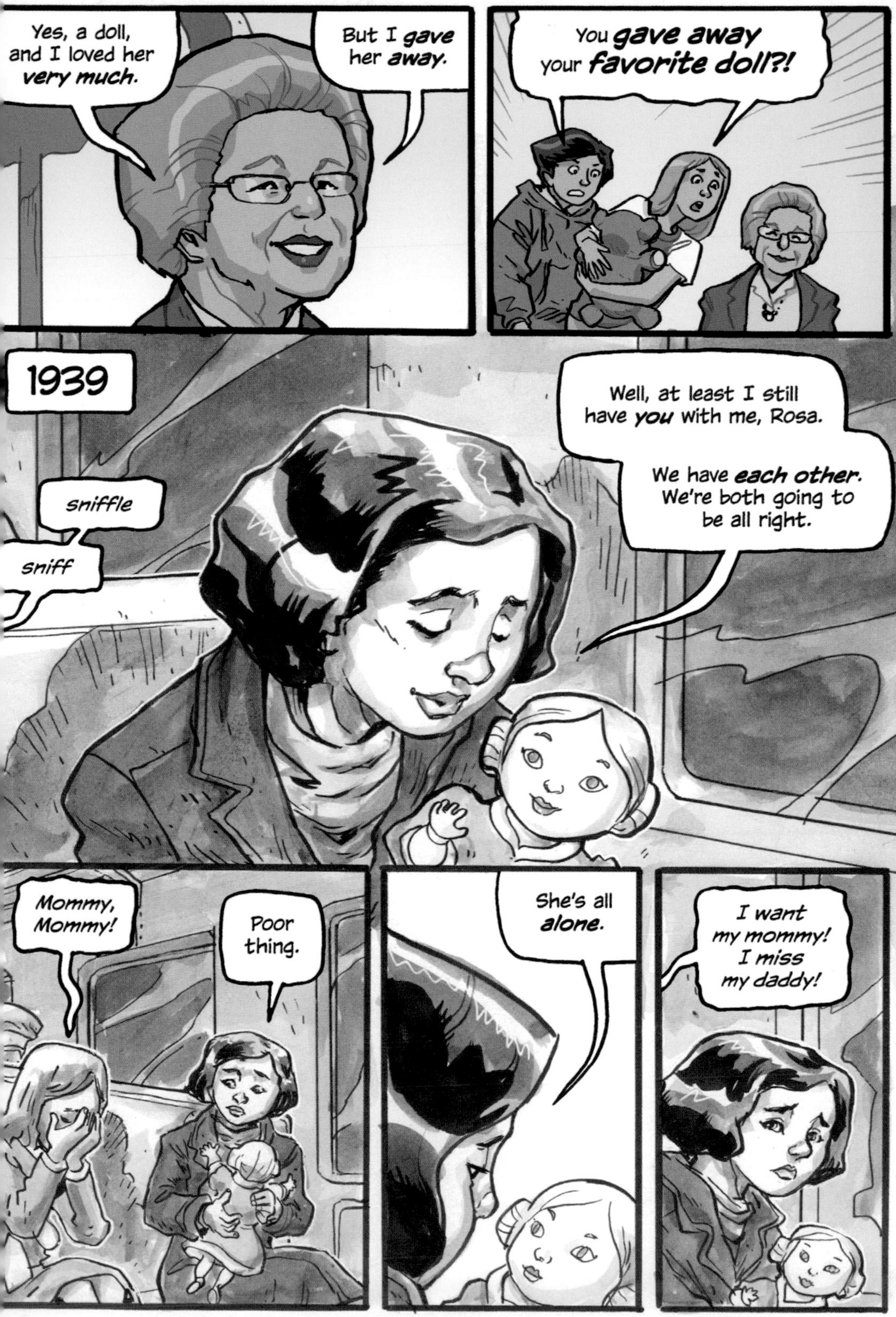
Yes, a doll, and I loved her *very much*.
But I *gave* her *away*.
You **gave away** your **favorite doll?!**
1939
Well, at least I still have ***you*** with me, Rosa.
We have ***each other***. We're both going to be all right.
sniffle
sniff
Mommy, Mommy!
Poor thing.
She's all ***alone***.
I want my mommy! I miss my daddy!

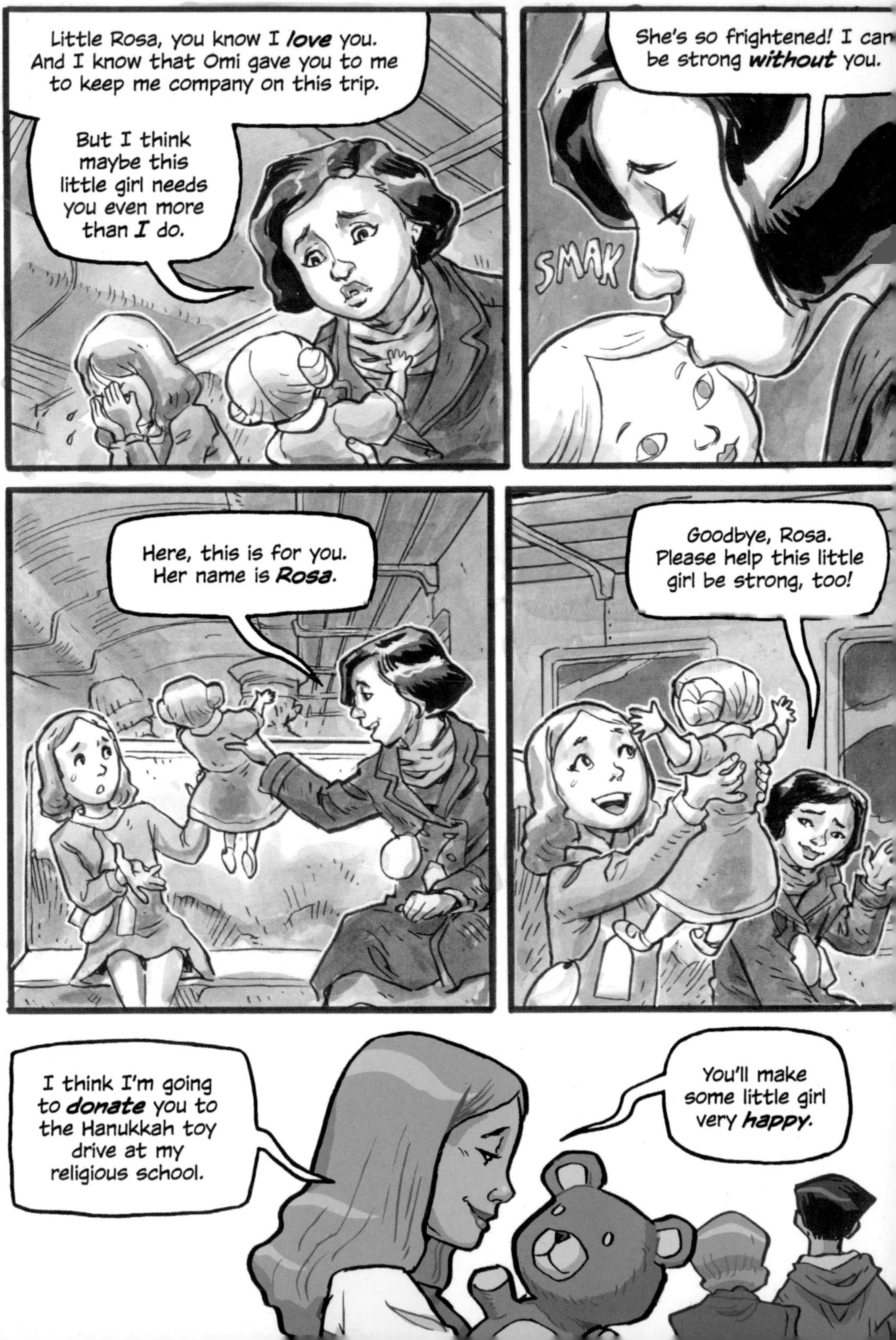
Little Rosa, you know I love you. And I know that Omi gave you to me to keep me company on this trip.
But I think maybe this little girl needs you even more than I do.
She's so frightened! I can be strong without you.
SMAK
Here, this is for you. Her name is Rosa.
Goodbye, Rosa. Please help this little girl be strong, too!
I think I'm going to donate you to the Hanukkah toy drive at my religious school.
You'll make some little girl very happy.

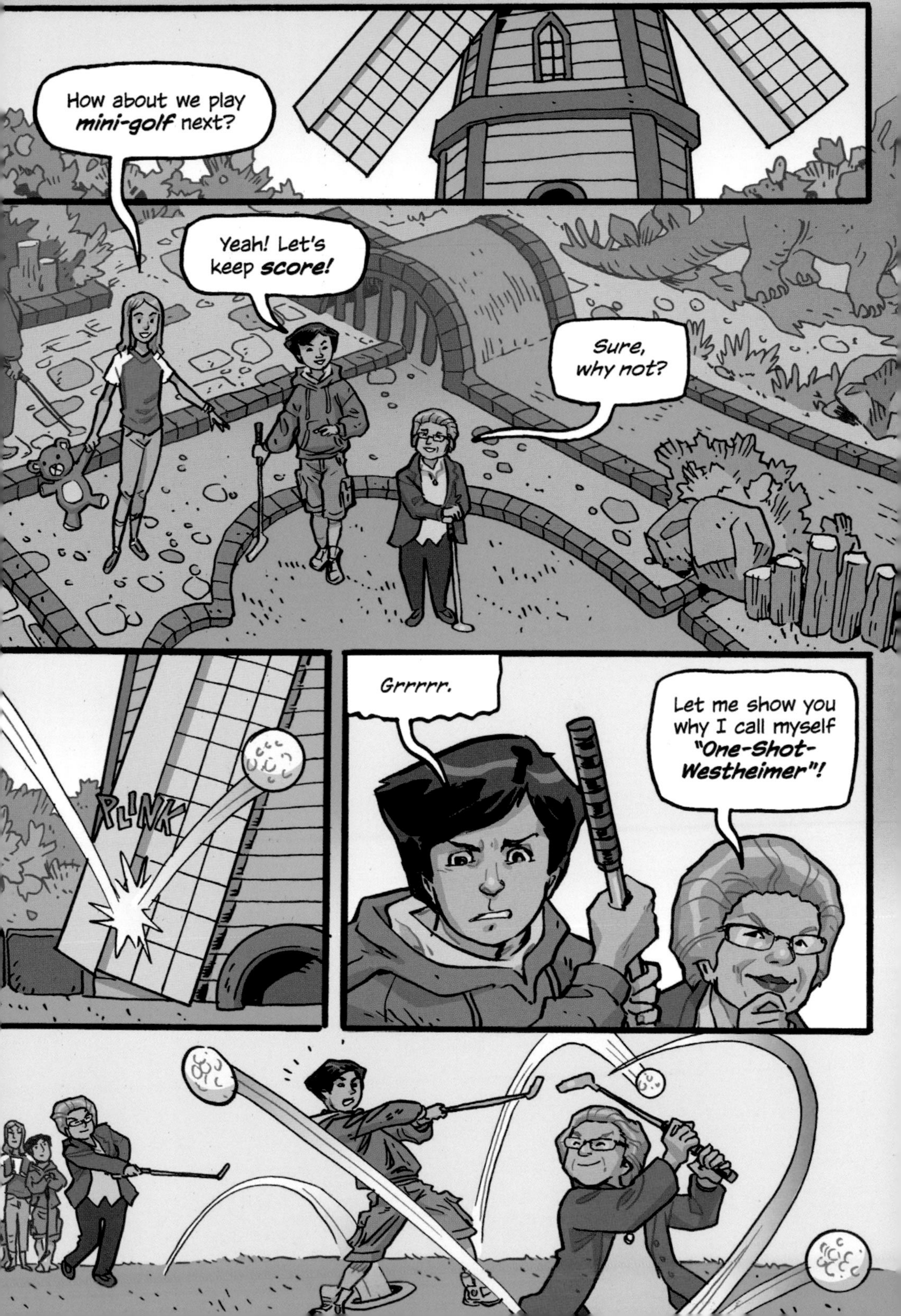
How about we play *mini-golf* next?
Yeah! Let's keep *score!*
Sure, why not?
PLINK
Grrrrr.
Let me show you why I call myself ***"One-Shot-Westheimer"!***

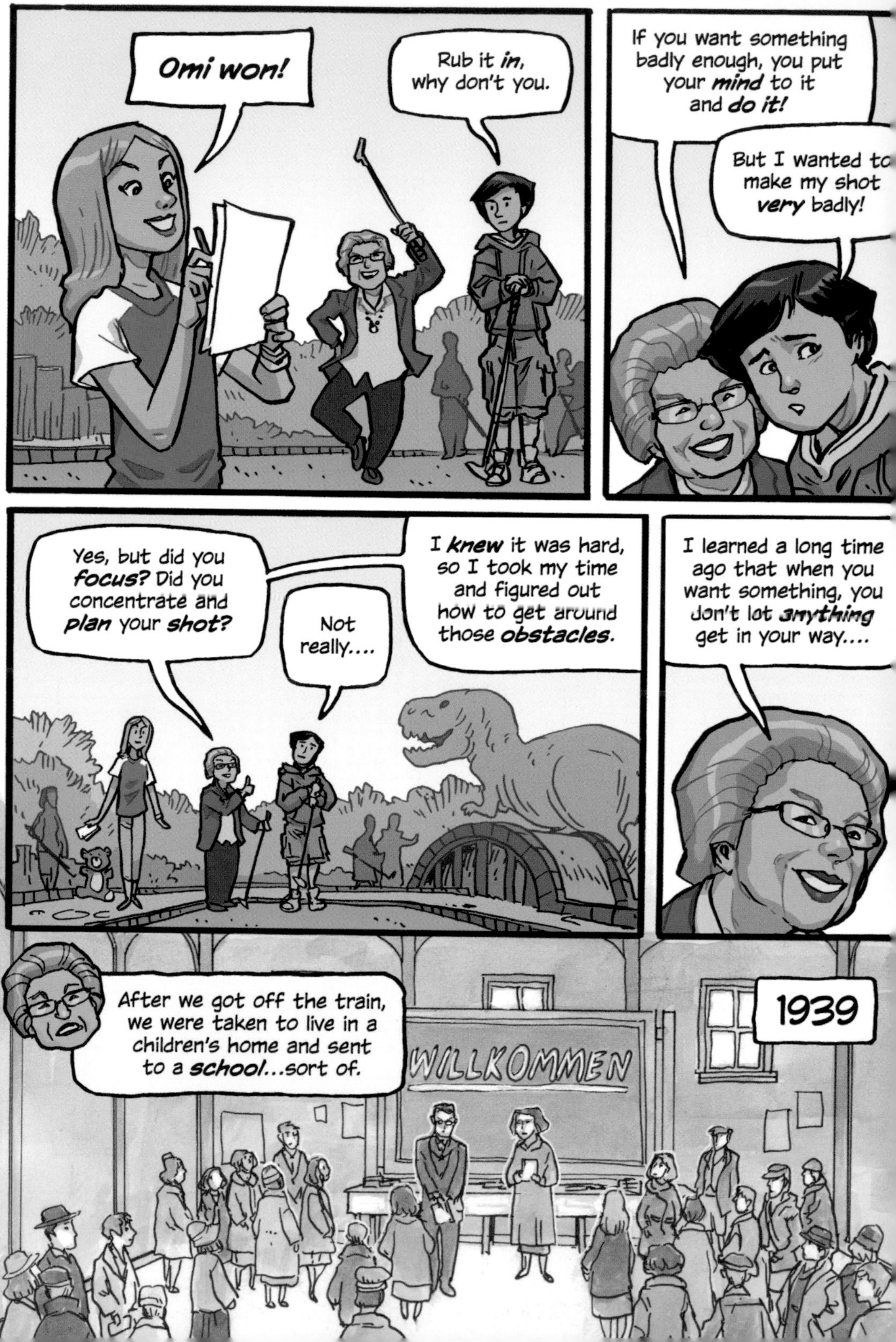
Omi won!
Rub it in, why don't you.
If you want something badly enough, you put your mind to it and do it!
But I wanted to make my shot very badly!
Yes, but did you focus? Did you concentrate and plan your shot?
Not really....
I knew it was hard, so I took my time and figured out how to get around those obstacles.
I learned a long time ago that when you want something, you don't let anything get in your way....
After we got off the train, we were taken to live in a children's home and sent to a school...sort of.
1939
WILLKOMMEN

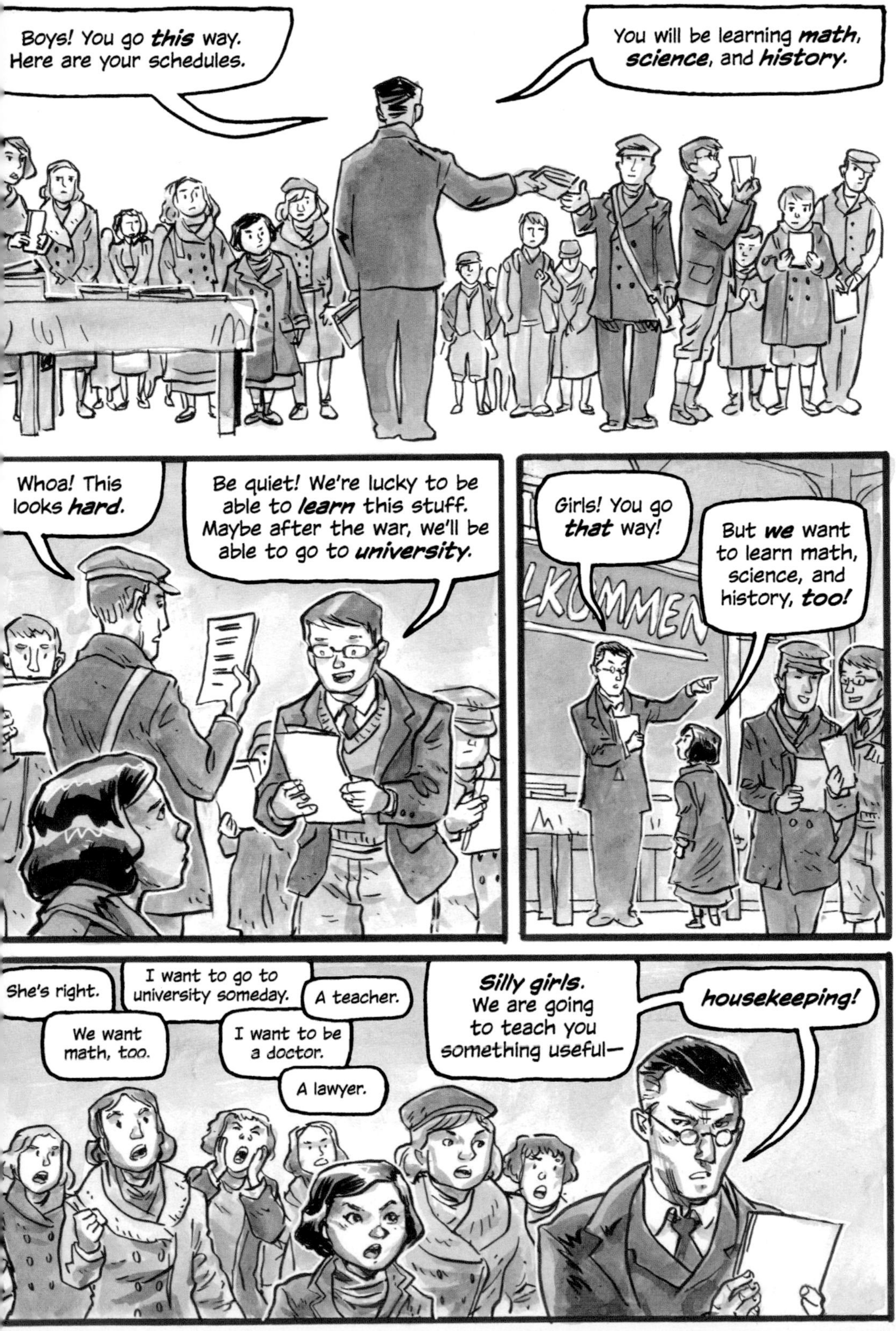

Boys! You go ***this*** way. Here are your schedules.
You will be learning ***math***, ***science***, and ***history***.
Whoa! This looks ***hard***.
Be quiet! We're lucky to be able to ***learn*** this stuff. Maybe after the war, we'll be able to go to ***university***.
Girls! You go ***that*** way!
LKOMMEN
But ***we*** want to learn math, science, and history, ***too!***
She's right.
I want to go to university someday.
A teacher.
We want math, too.
I want to be a doctor.
A lawyer.
Silly girls. We are going to teach you something useful—
housekeeping!

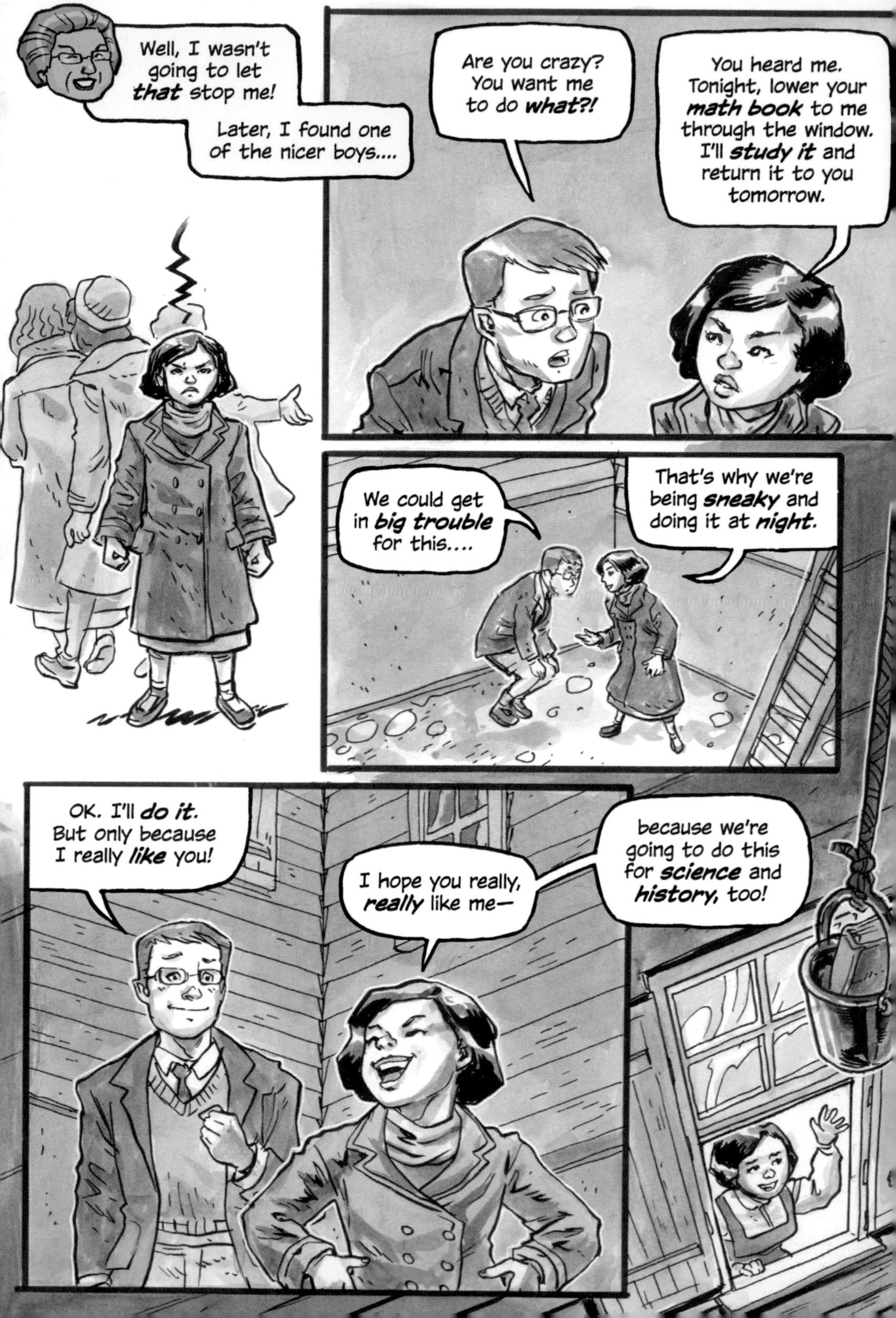

Well, I wasn't going to let *that* stop me!
Later, I found one of the nicer boys....
Are you crazy? You want me to do *what?!*
You heard me. Tonight, lower your *math book* to me through the window. I'll *study it* and return it to you tomorrow.
We could get in *big trouble* for this....
That's why we're being *sneaky* and doing it at *night*.
OK. I'll *do it*. But only because I really *like* you!
I hope you really, *really* like me—
because we're going to do this for *science* and *history*, too!

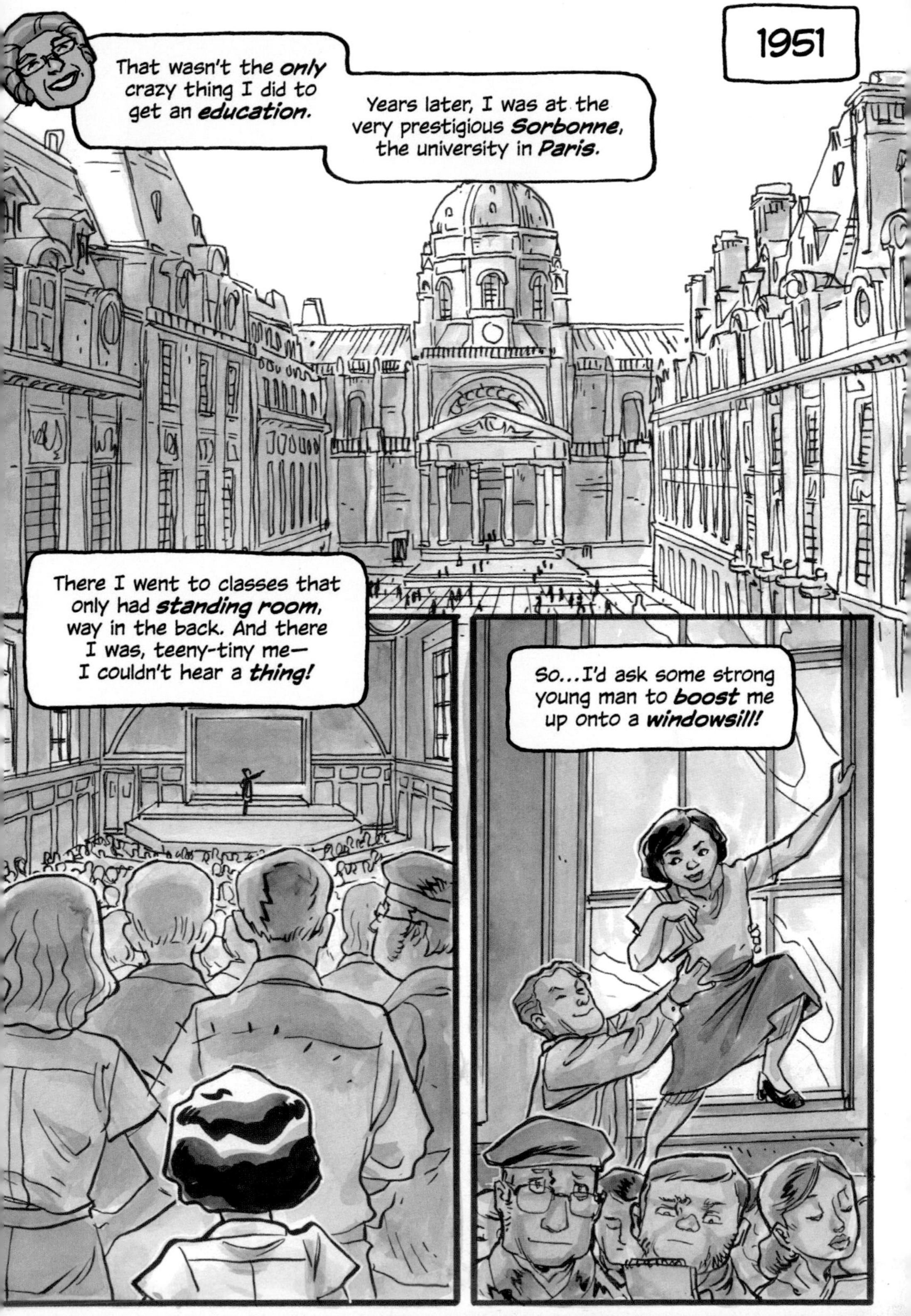
1951
That wasn't the only crazy thing I did to get an education.
Years later, I was at the very prestigious Sorbonne, the university in Paris.
There I went to classes that only had standing room, way in the back. And there I was, teeny-tiny me— I couldn't hear a thing!
So...I'd ask some strong young man to boost me up onto a windowsill!

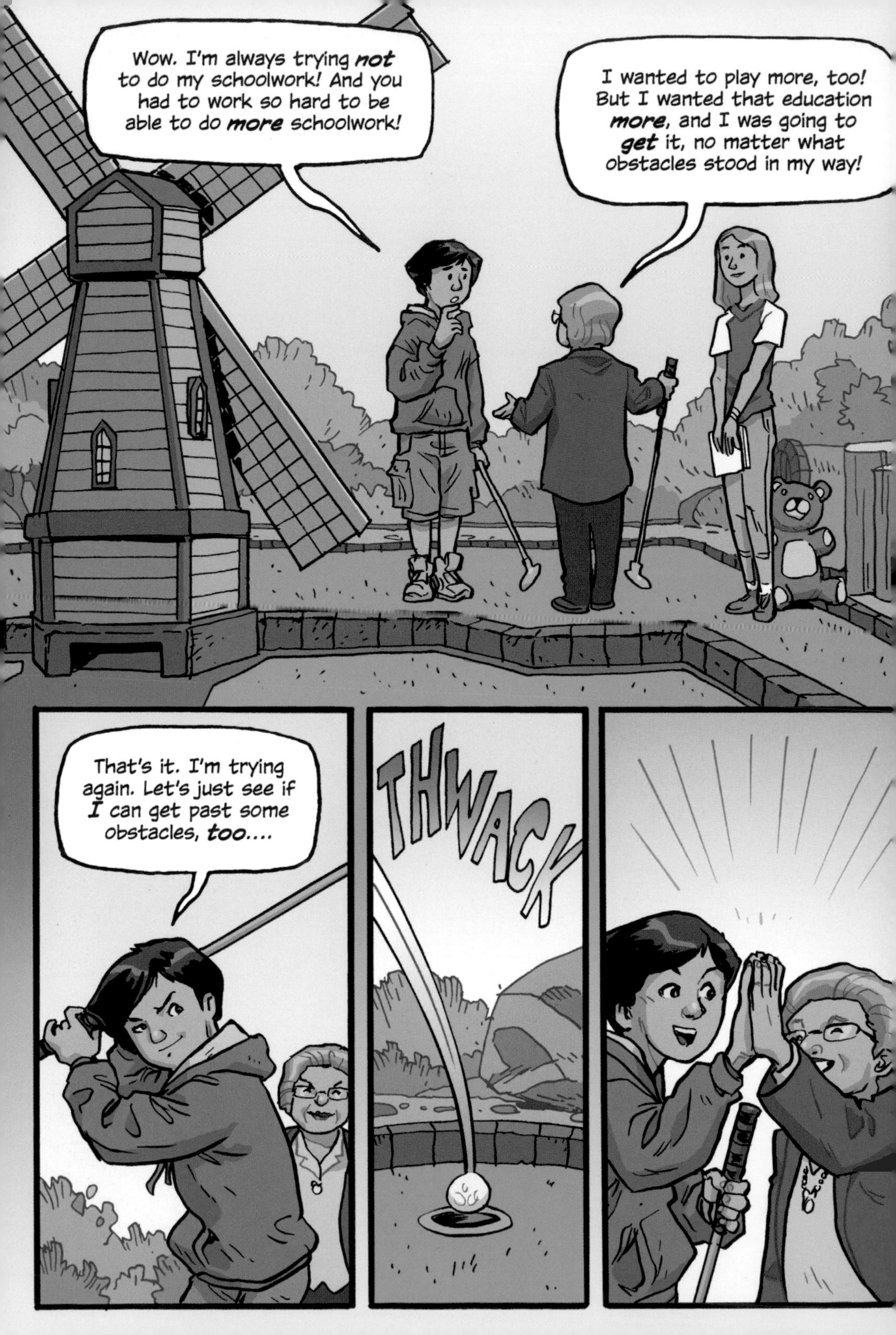
Wow. I'm always trying *not* to do my schoolwork! And you had to work so hard to be able to do *more* schoolwork!
I wanted to play more, too! But I wanted that education *more*, and I was going to *get* it, no matter what obstacles stood in my way!
That's it. I'm trying again. Let's just see if *I* can get past some obstacles, *too*....
THWACK

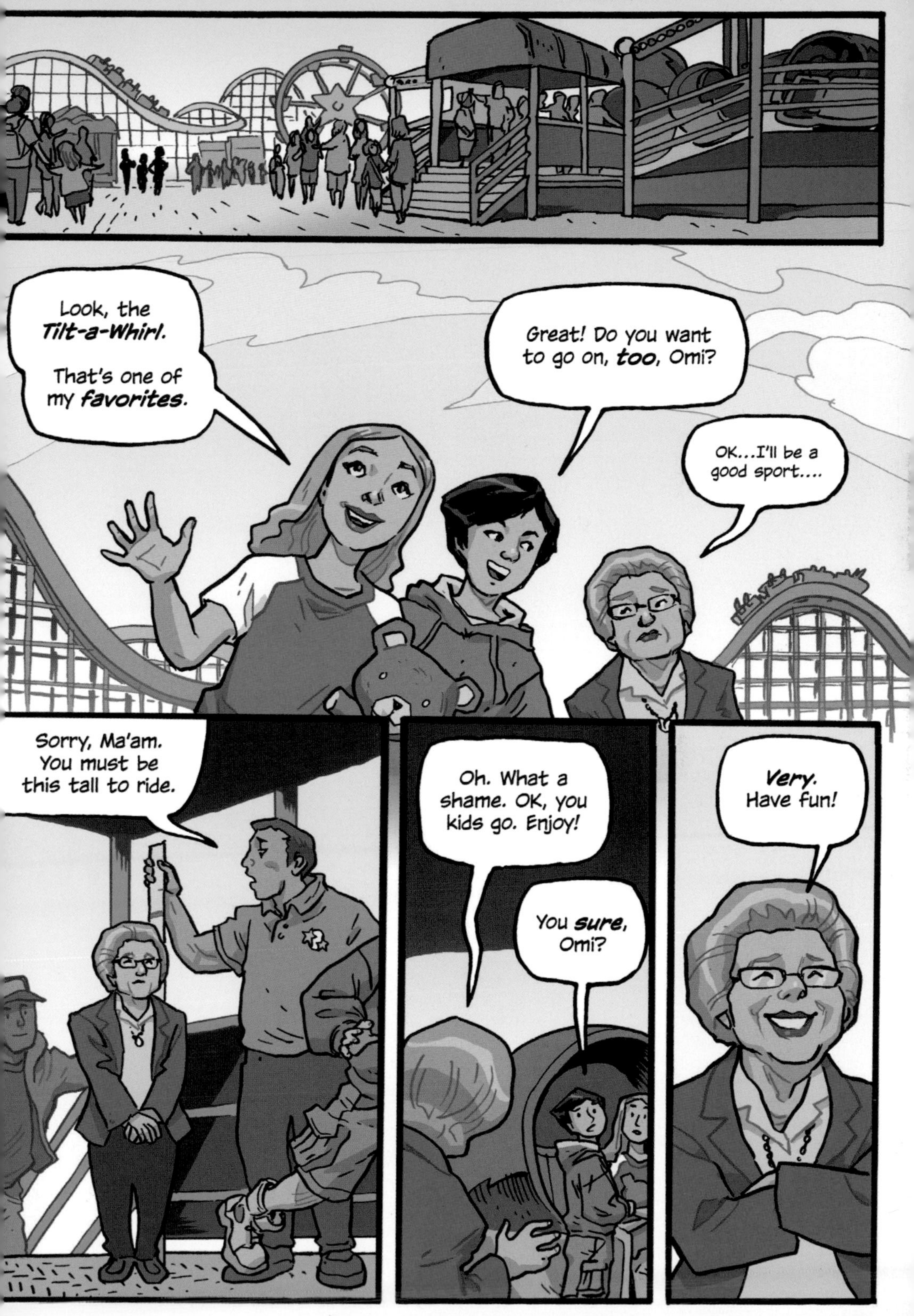
Look, the *Tilt-a-Whirl*.
That's one of my *favorites*.
Great! Do you want to go on, *too*, Omi?
OK...I'll be a good sport....
Sorry, Ma'am. You must be this tall to ride.
Oh. What a shame. OK, you kids go. Enjoy!
You *sure*, Omi?
Very. Have fun!

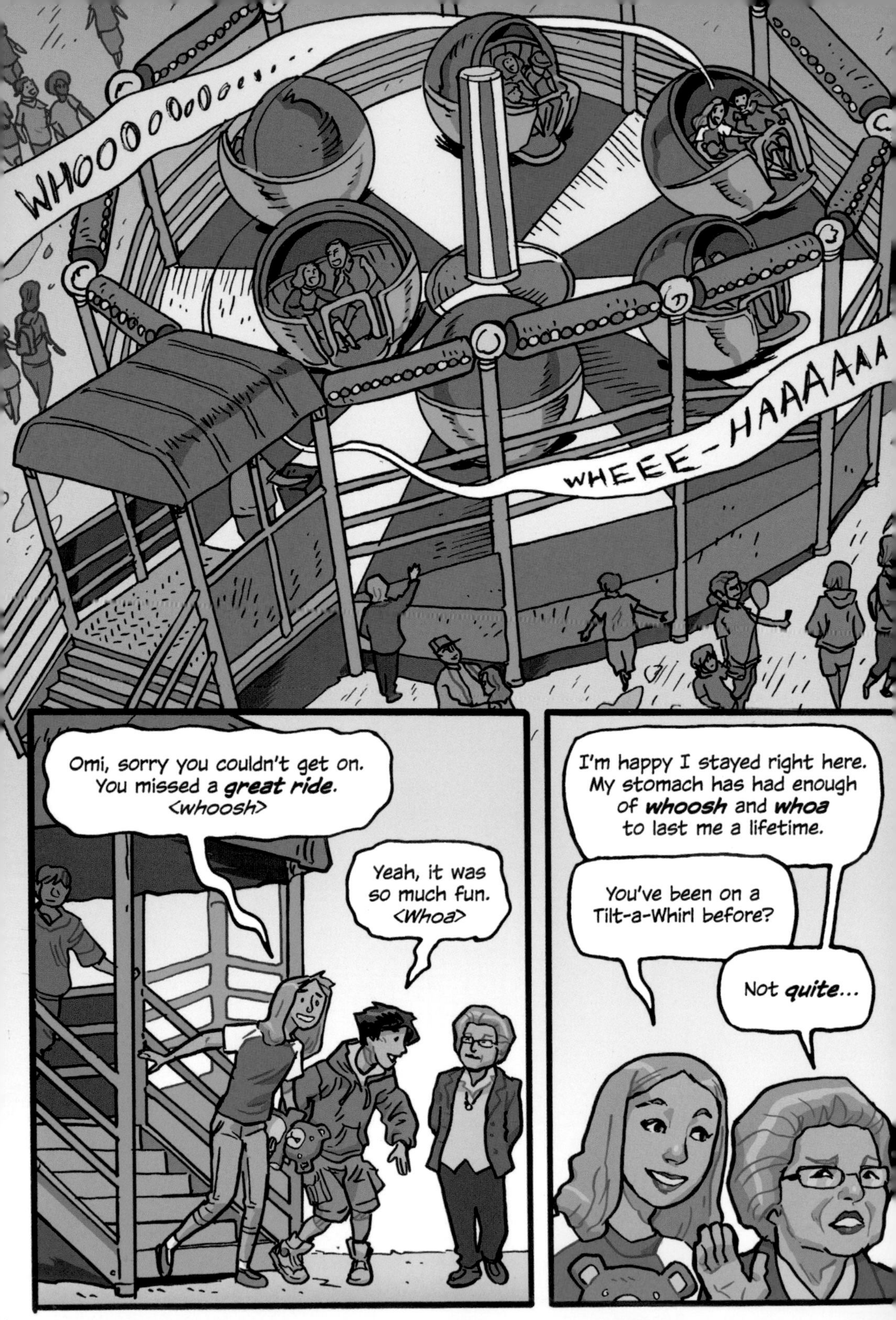
WHOOOOOOOooeu...
WHEEE-HAAAAAA
Omi, sorry you couldn't get on. You missed a *great ride*. <whoosh>
Yeah, it was so much fun. <Whoa>
I'm happy I stayed right here. My stomach has had enough of *whoosh* and *whoa* to last me a lifetime.
You've been on a Tilt-a-Whirl before?
Not *quite*...

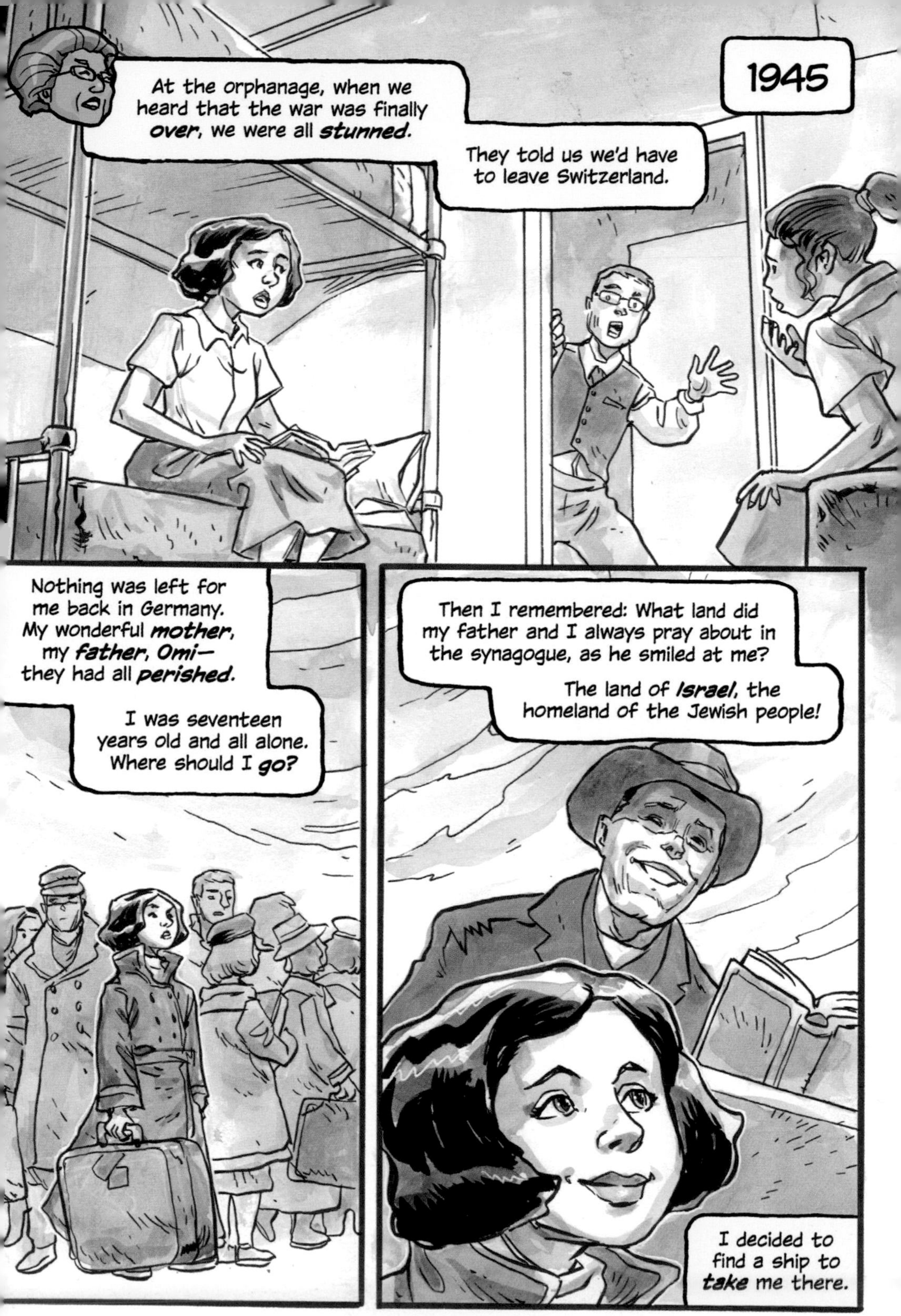
1945
At the orphanage, when we heard that the war was finally *over*, we were all *stunned*.
They told us we'd have to leave Switzerland.
Nothing was left for me back in Germany. My wonderful *mother*, my *father*, Omi— they had all *perished*.
I was seventeen years old and all alone. Where should I *go?*
Then I remembered: What land did my father and I always pray about in the synagogue, as he smiled at me?
The land of *Israel*, the homeland of the Jewish people!
I decided to find a ship to *take* me there.

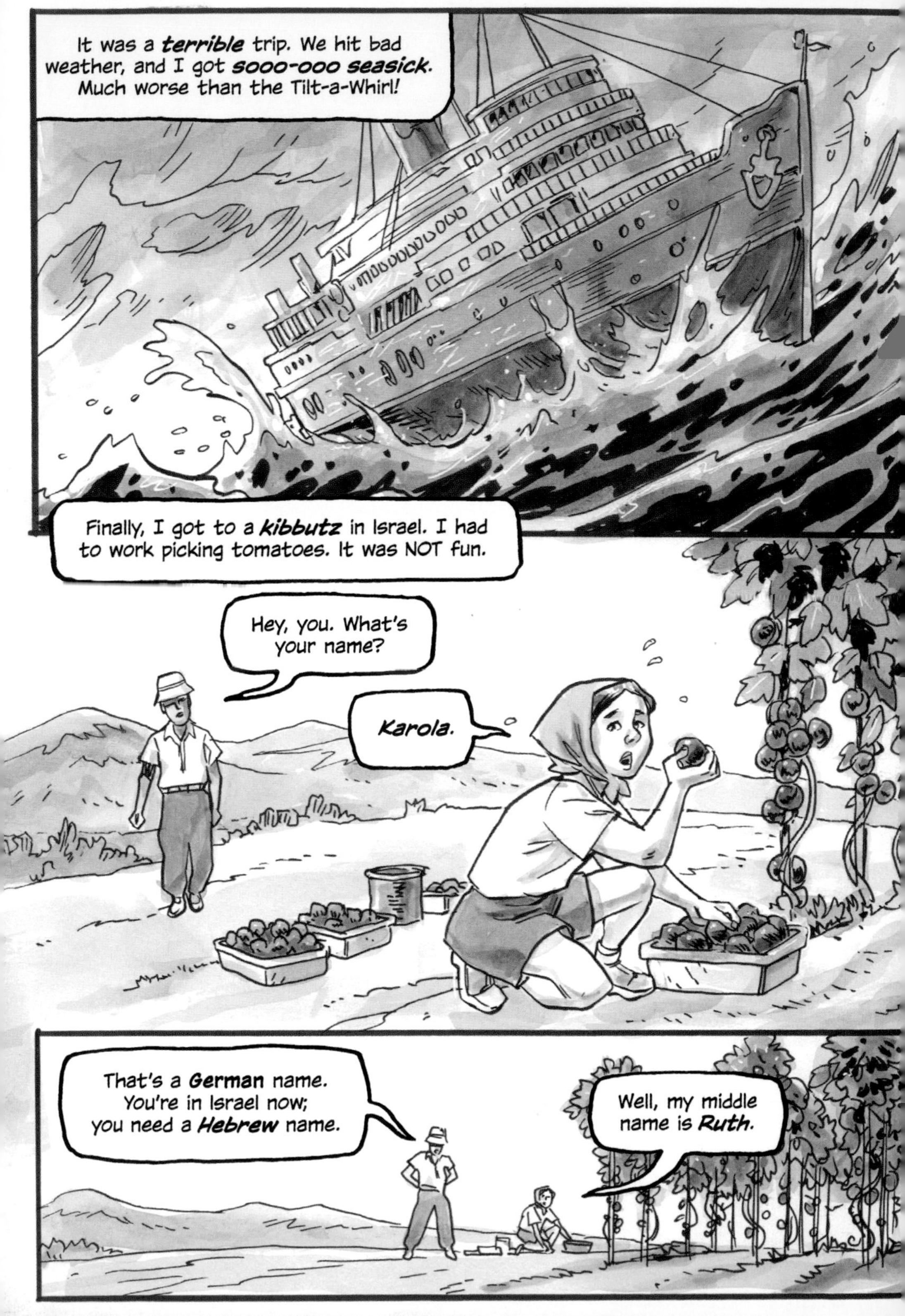
It was a *terrible* trip. We hit bad weather, and I got *sooo-ooo seasick*. Much worse than the Tilt-a-Whirl!
Finally, I got to a *kibbutz* in Israel. I had to work picking tomatoes. It was NOT fun.
Hey, you. What's your name?
Karola.
That's a **German** name. You're in Israel now; you need a *Hebrew* name.
Well, my middle name is *Ruth*.

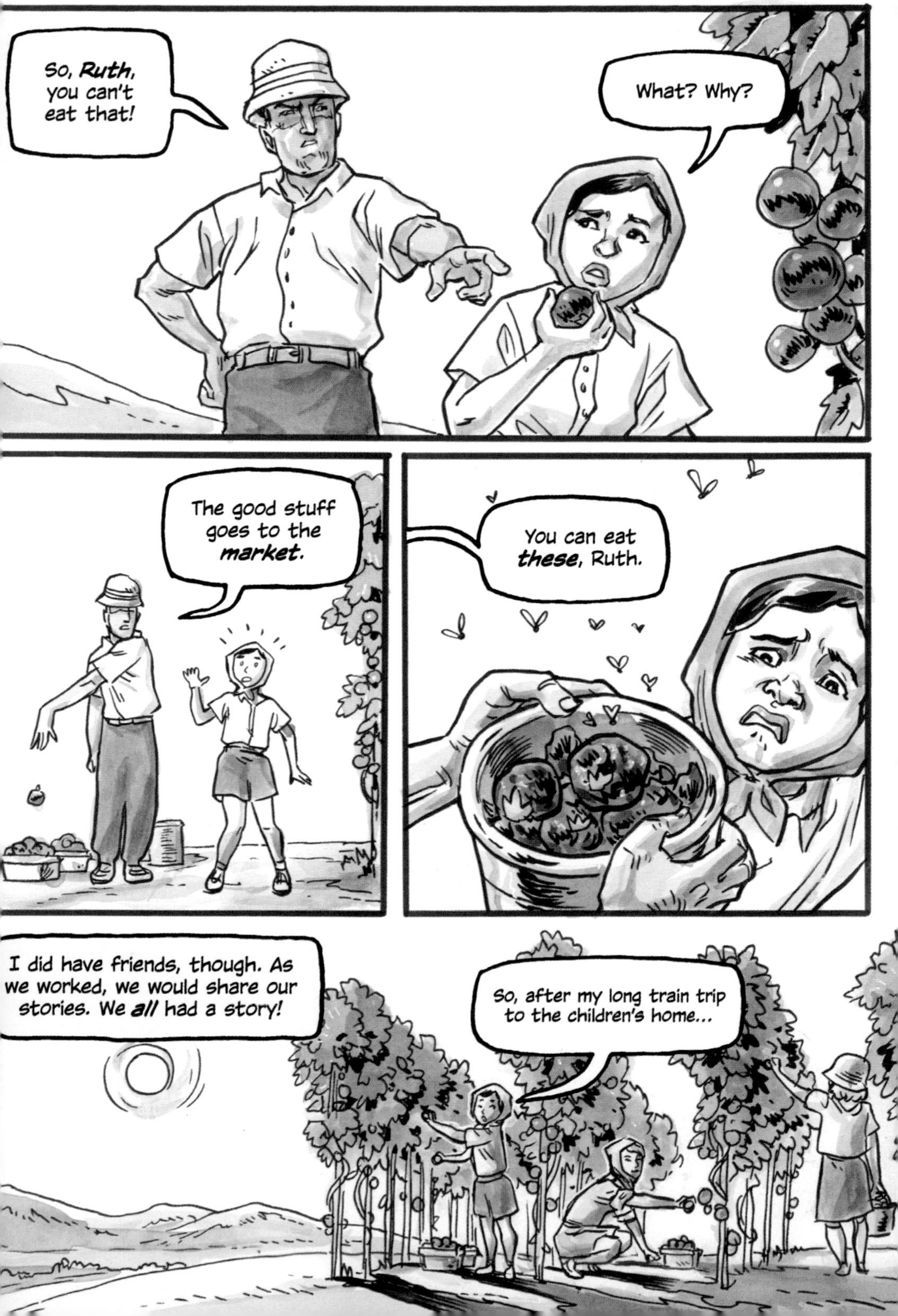
So, Ruth, you can't eat that!
What? Why?
The good stuff goes to the market.
You can eat these, Ruth.
I did have friends, though. As we worked, we would share our stories. We all had a story!
So, after my long train trip to the children's home...

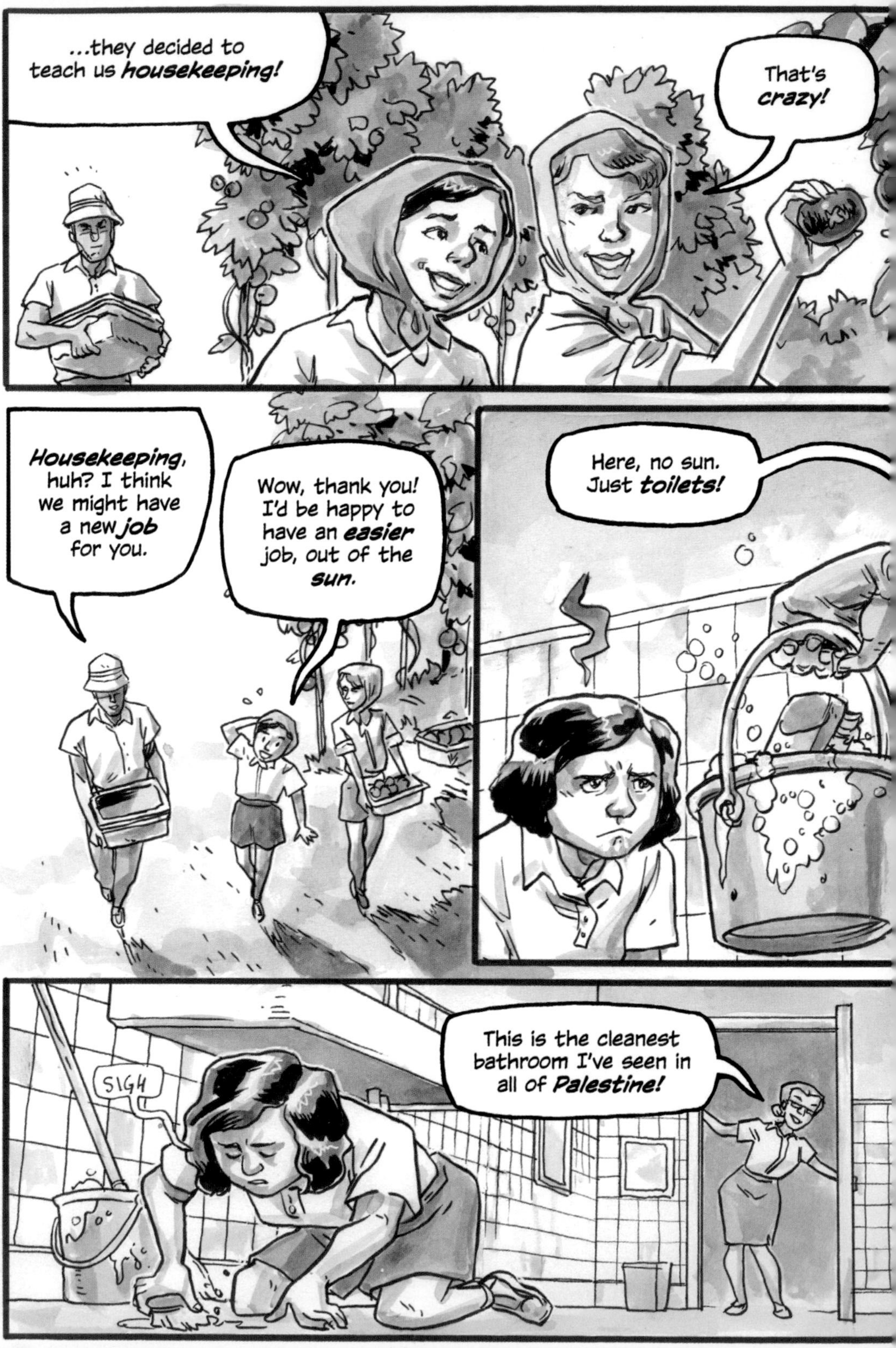
...they decided to teach us *housekeeping!*
That's *crazy!*
Housekeeping, huh? I think we might have a new *job* for you.
Wow, thank you! I'd be happy to have an *easier* job, out of the *sun*.
Here, no sun. Just *toilets!*
SIGH
This is the cleanest bathroom I've seen in all of *Palestine!*

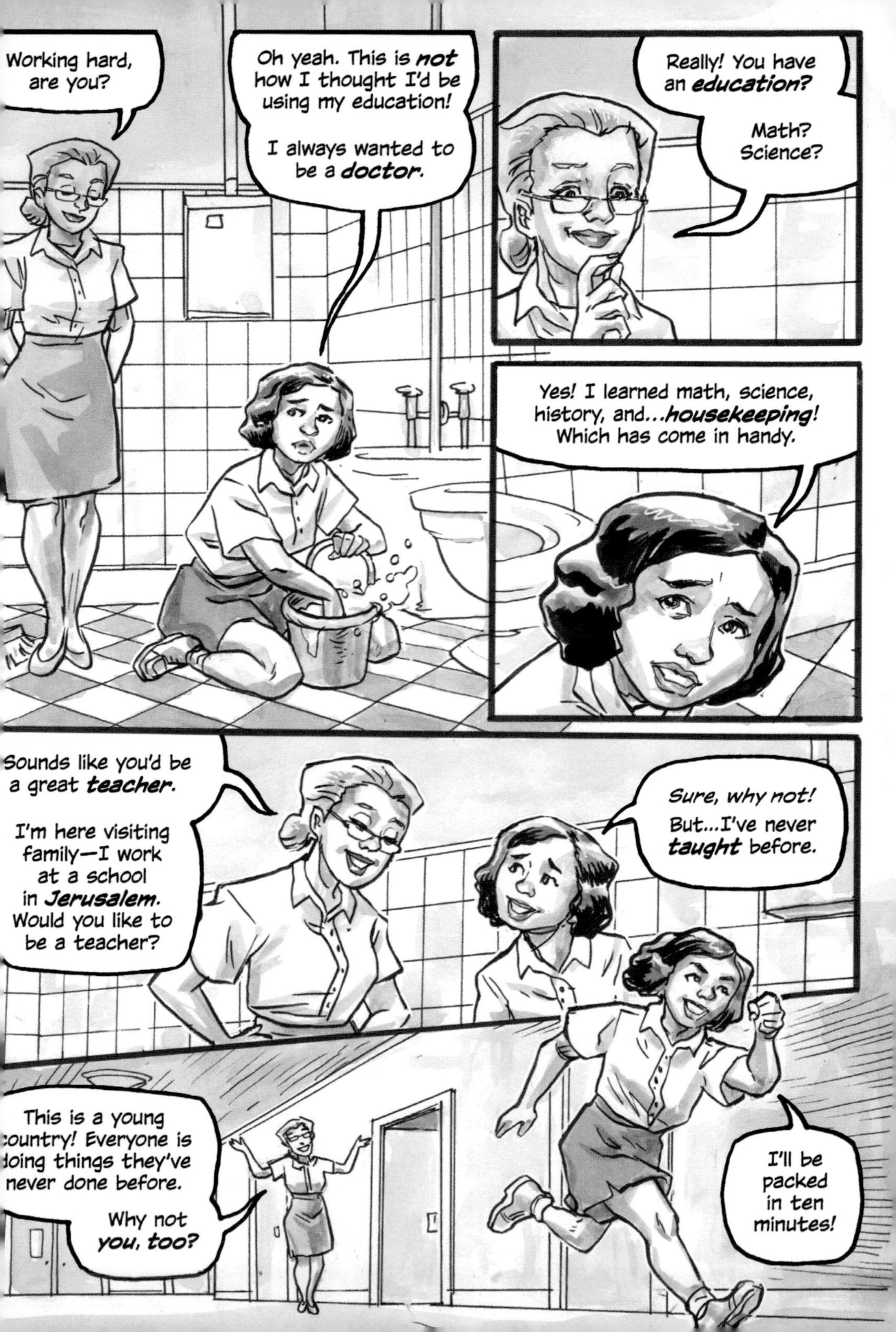

Working hard, are you?
Oh yeah. This is not how I thought I'd be using my education!
I always wanted to be a doctor.
Really! You have an education?
Math? Science?
Yes! I learned math, science, history, and...housekeeping! Which has come in handy.
Sounds like you'd be a great teacher.
I'm here visiting family—I work at a school in Jerusalem. Would you like to be a teacher?
Sure, why not!
But...I've never taught before.
This is a young country! Everyone is doing things they've never done before.
Why not you, too?
I'll be packed in ten minutes!

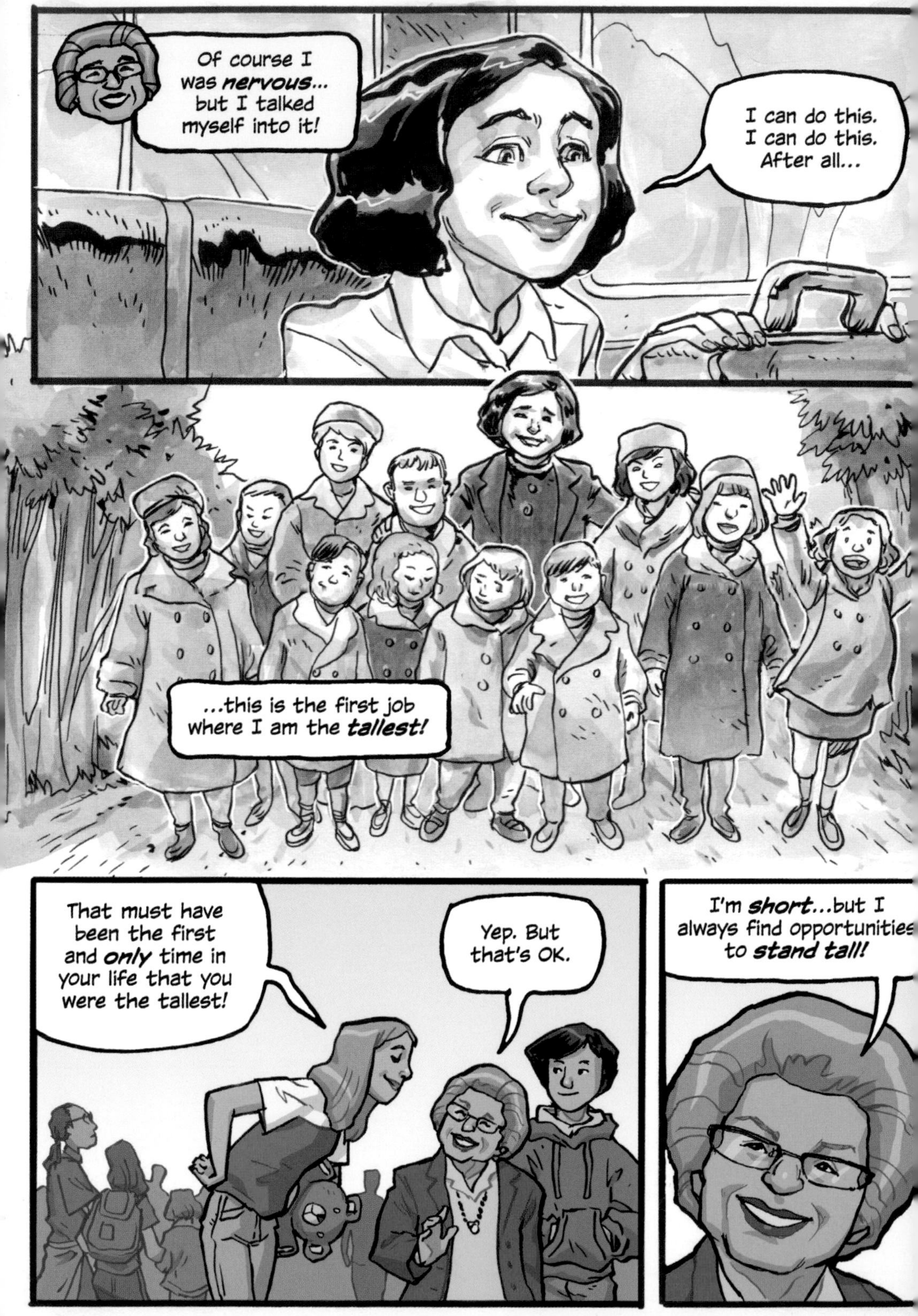
Of course I was nervous... but I talked myself into it!
I can do this. I can do this. After all...
...this is the first job where I am the tallest!
That must have been the first and only time in your life that you were the tallest!
Yep. But that's OK.
I'm short...but I always find opportunities to stand tall!

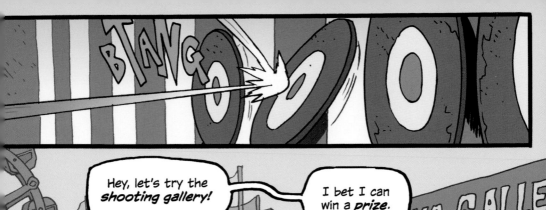

Hey, let's try the _shooting gallery!_

I bet I can win a _prize._

Sorry, guns are not a _game_ to me.

Why? Scared you're not as good at _shooting_ as you are at _mini-golf?_

I happen to be a _very good_ shot....

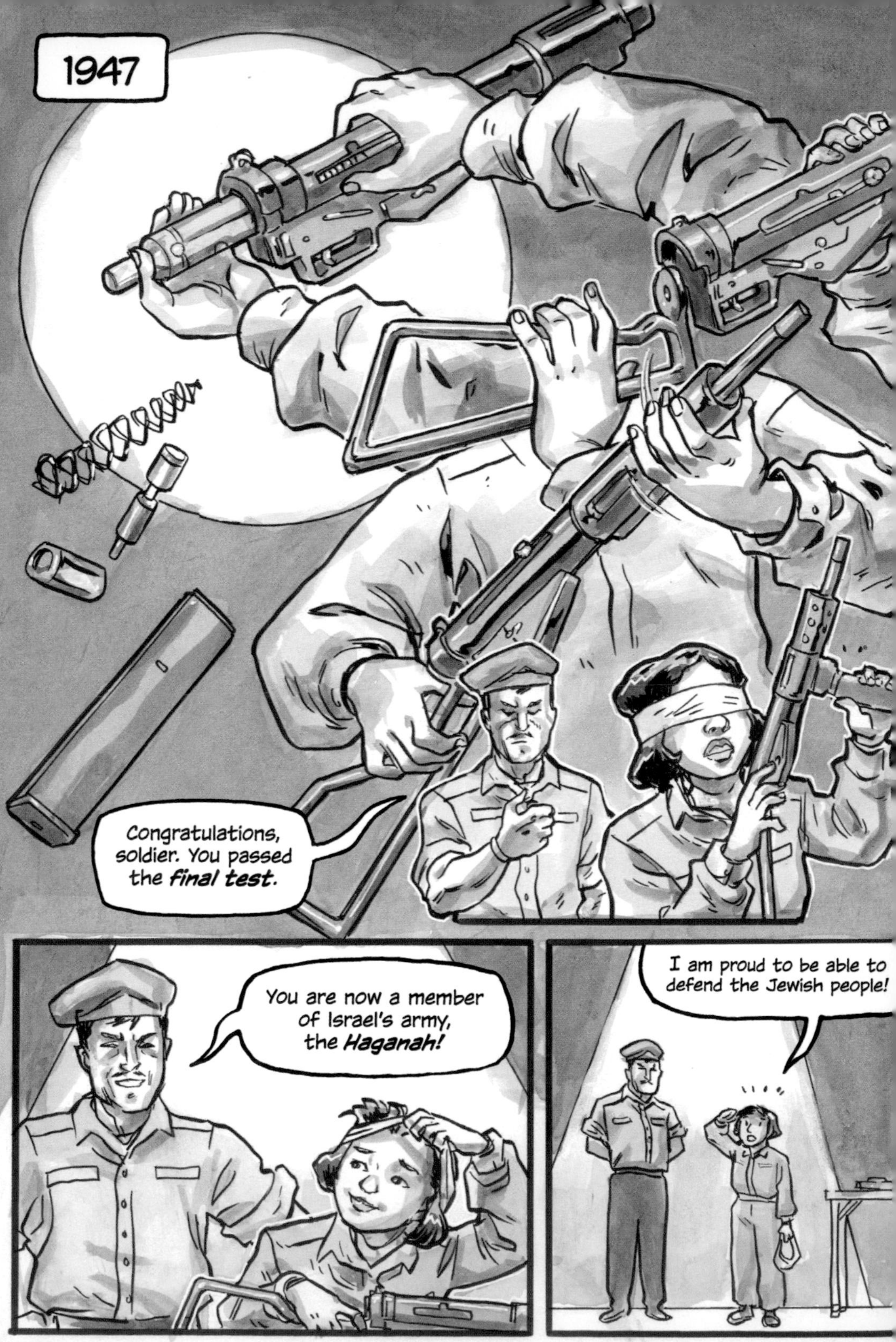
1947
Congratulations, soldier. You passed the *final test*.
You are now a member of Israel's army, the *Haganah!*
I am proud to be able to defend the Jewish people!

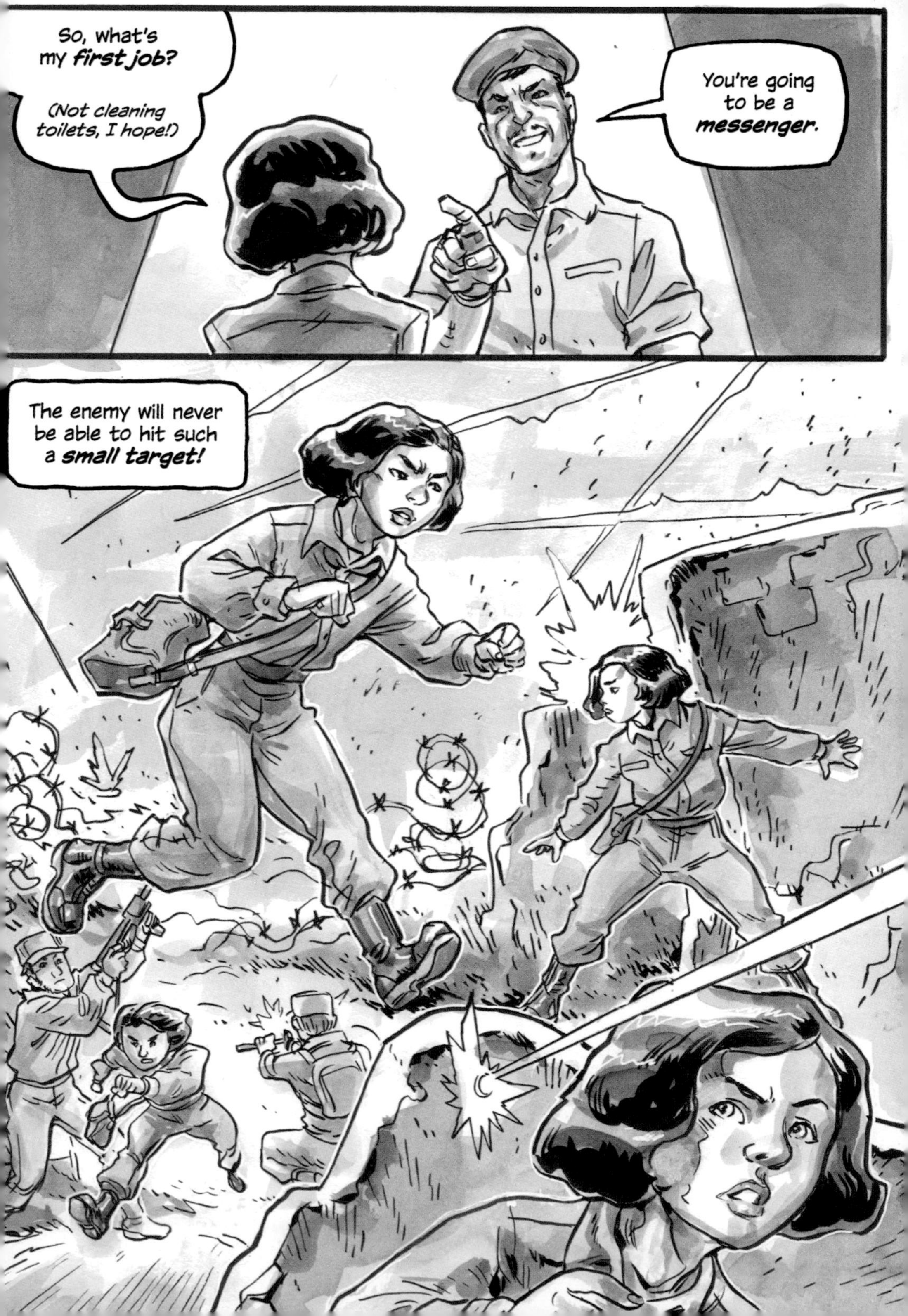
So, what's my *first job?*
(Not cleaning toilets, I hope!)
You're going to be a *messenger*.
The enemy will never be able to hit such a *small target!*

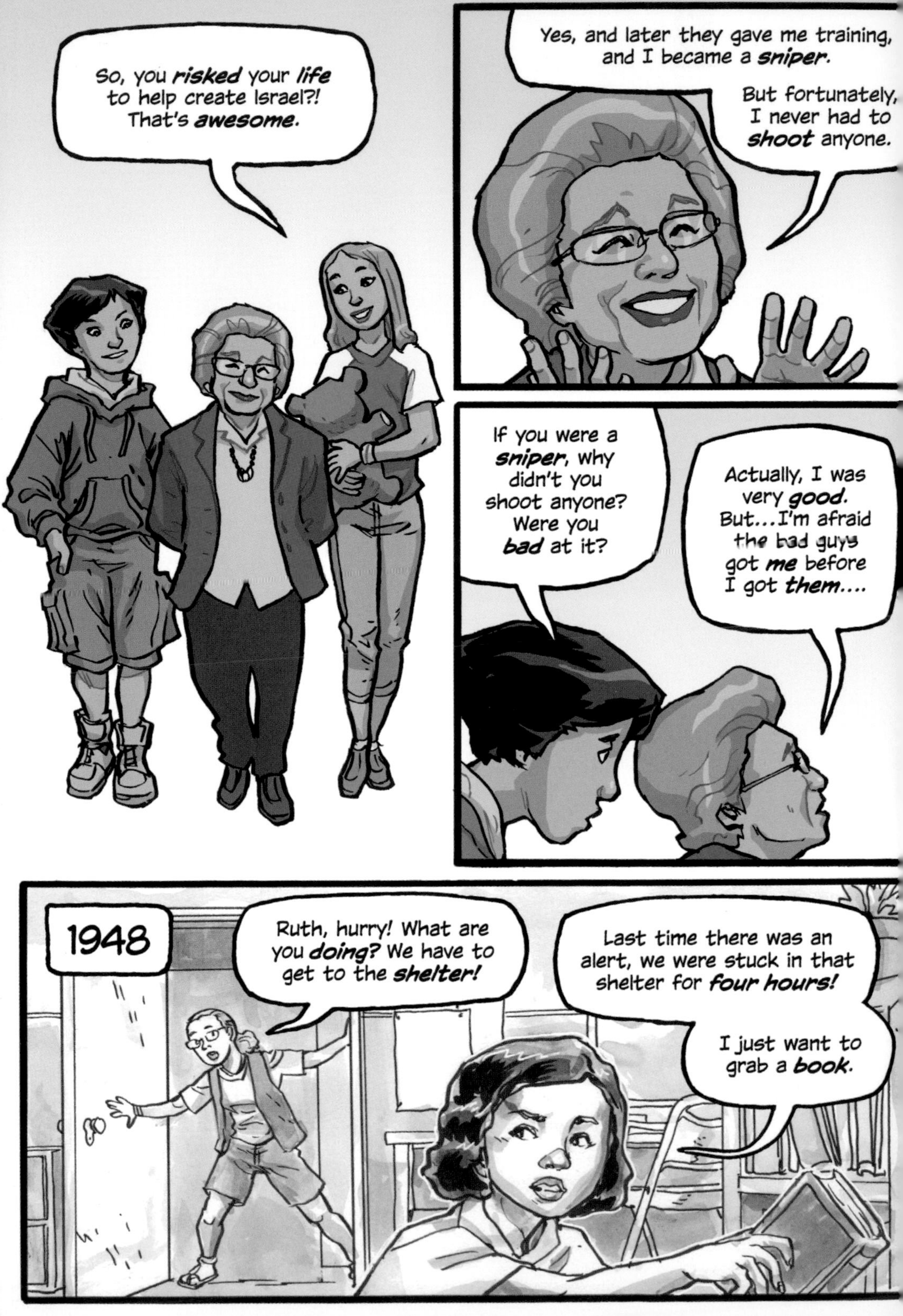
So, you **risked** your **life** to help create Israel?! That's **awesome**.
Yes, and later they gave me training, and I became a **sniper**.
But fortunately, I never had to **shoot** anyone.
If you were a **sniper**, why didn't you shoot anyone? Were you **bad** at it?
Actually, I was very **good**. But...I'm afraid the bad guys got **me** before I got **them**....
1948
Ruth, hurry! What are you **doing?** We have to get to the **shelter!**
Last time there was an alert, we were stuck in that shelter for **four hours!**
I just want to grab a **book**.

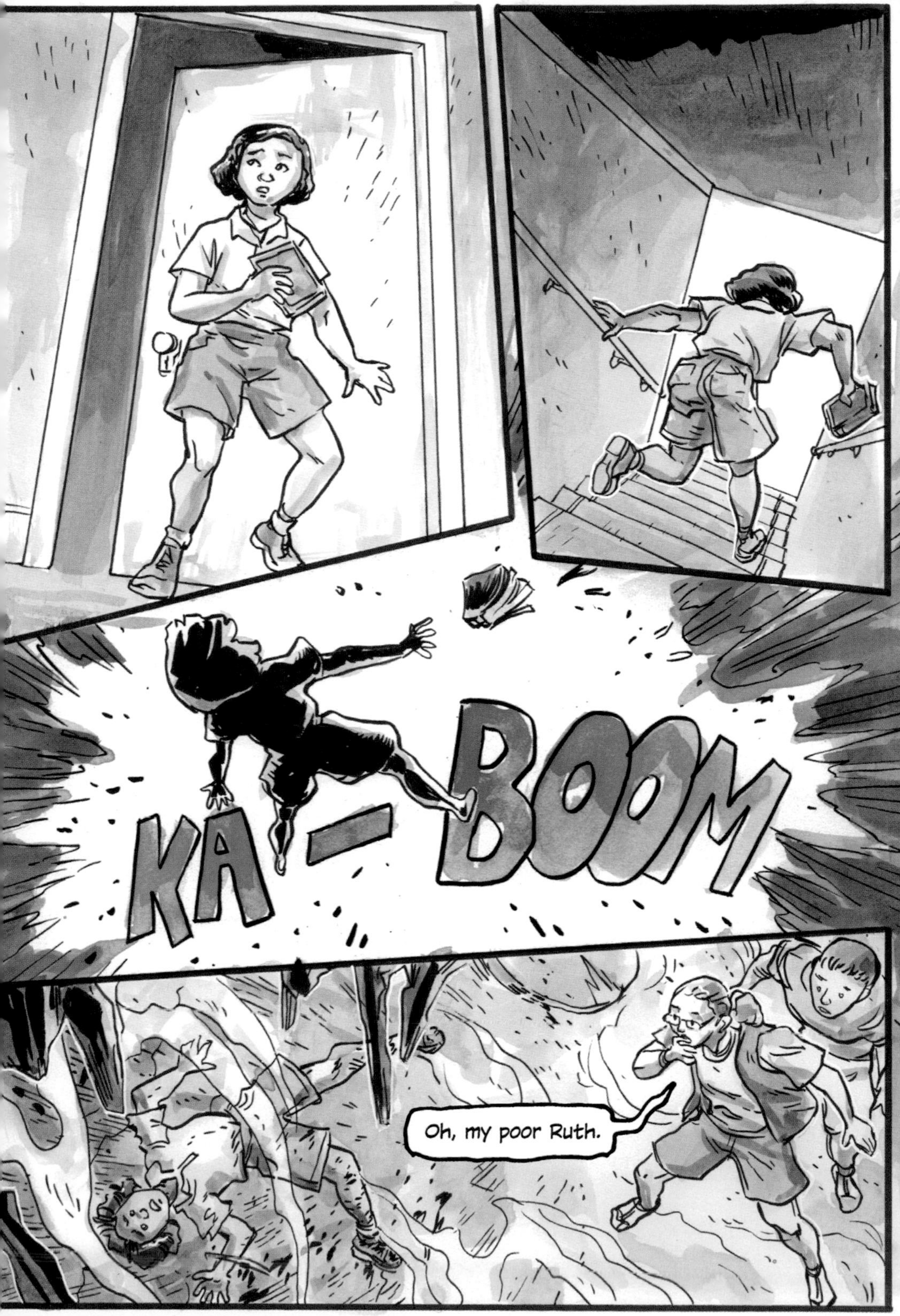
KA-BOOM
Oh, my poor Ruth.

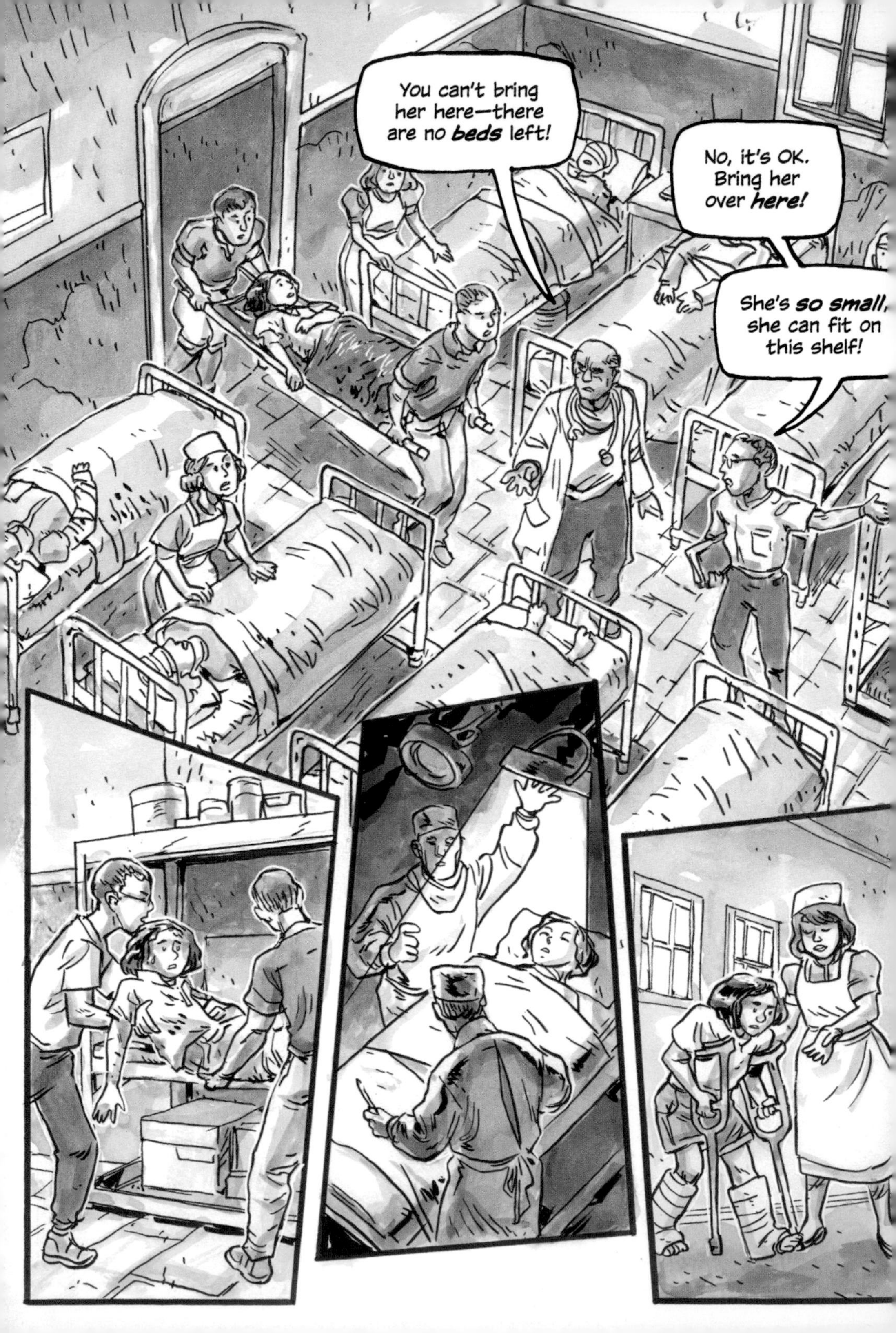
You can't bring her here—there are no beds left!
No, it's OK. Bring her over here!
She's so small, she can fit on this shelf!

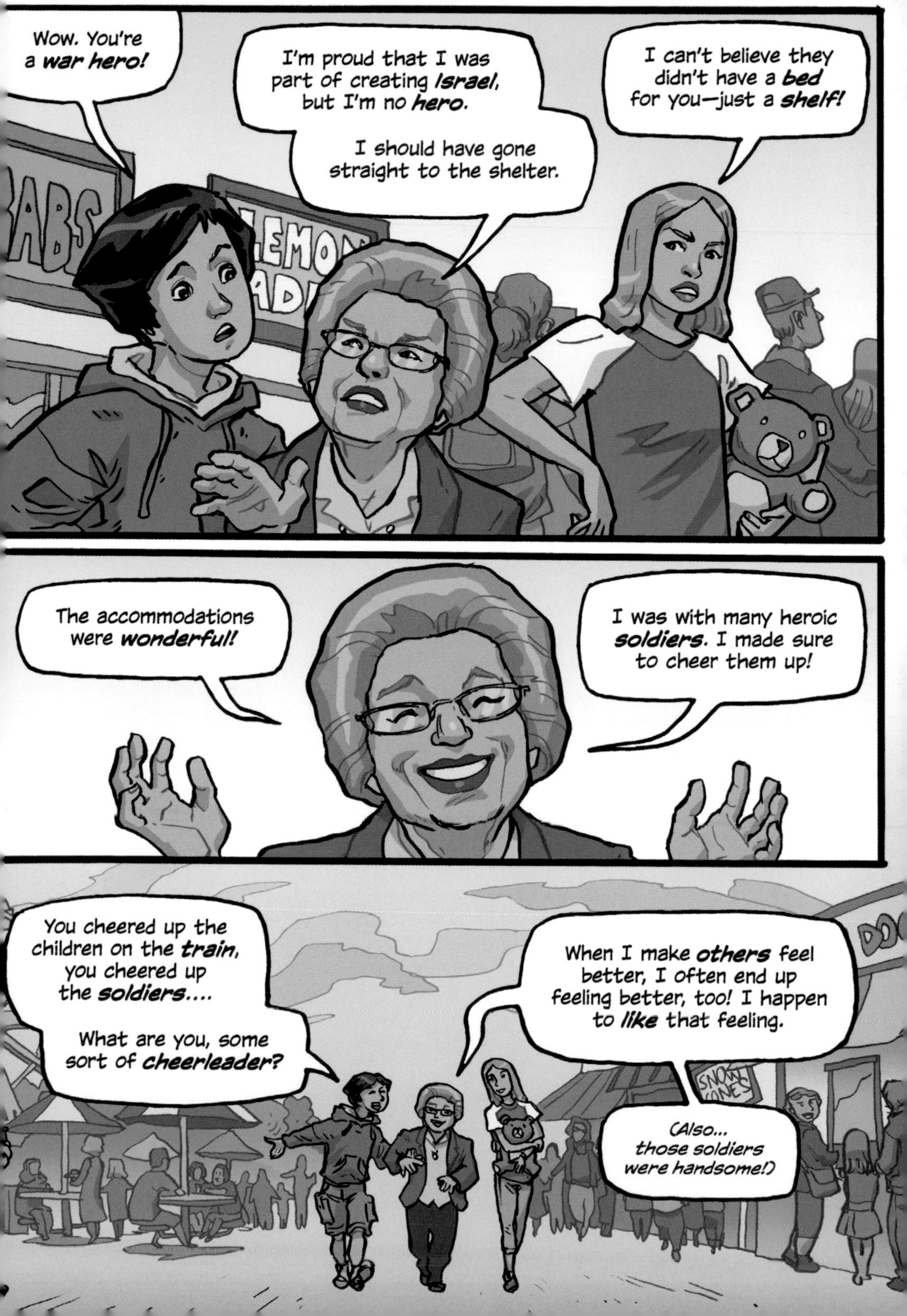

Wow. You're a **war hero!**
I'm proud that I was part of creating *Israel*, but I'm no **hero**.
I should have gone straight to the shelter.
I can't believe they didn't have a **bed** for you—just a **shelf!**
The accommodations were **wonderful!**
I was with many heroic **soldiers**. I made sure to cheer them up!
You cheered up the children on the **train**, you cheered up the **soldiers**....
What are you, some sort of **cheerleader?**
When I make **others** feel better, I often end up feeling better, too! I happen to **like** that feeling.
(Also... those soldiers were handsome!)
SNOW CONES

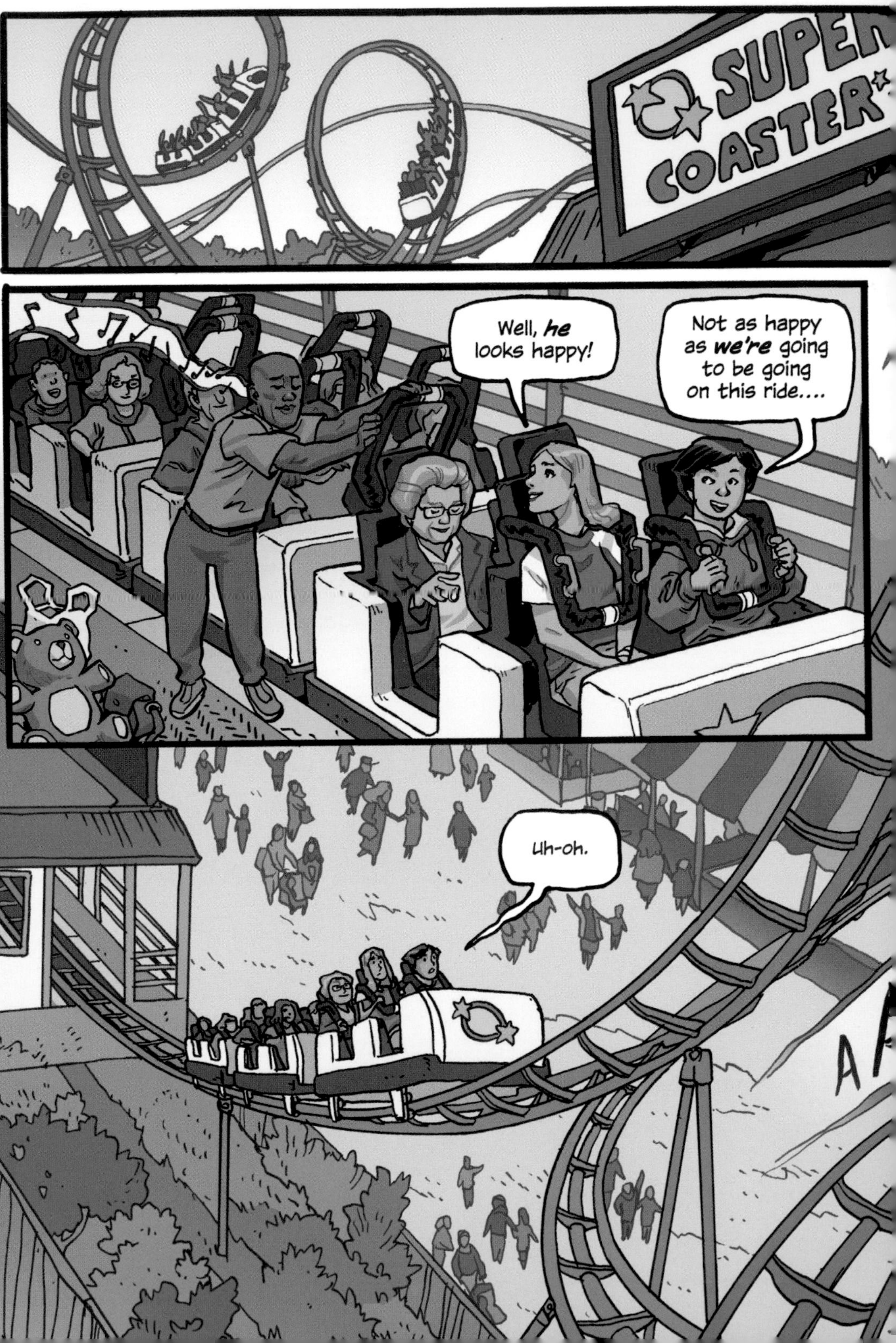
SUPER
COASTER
Well, he looks happy!
Not as happy as we're going to be going on this ride....
Uh-oh.

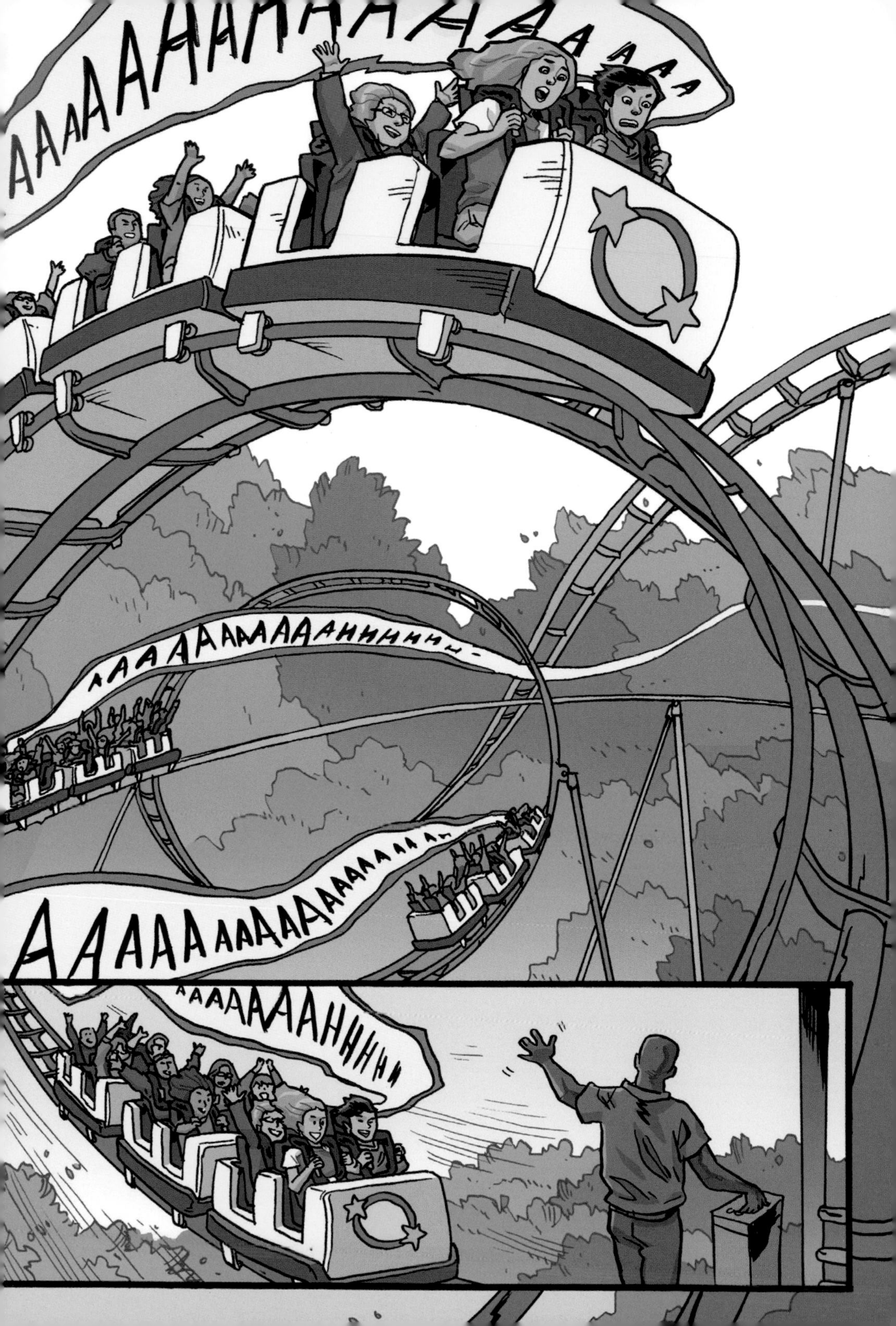
AAAAAAHHHHHHAAAAAAA
AAAAAAAAAHHHHHHH-
AAAAAAAAAAAAAAAAAA
AAAAAAAHHHHHH

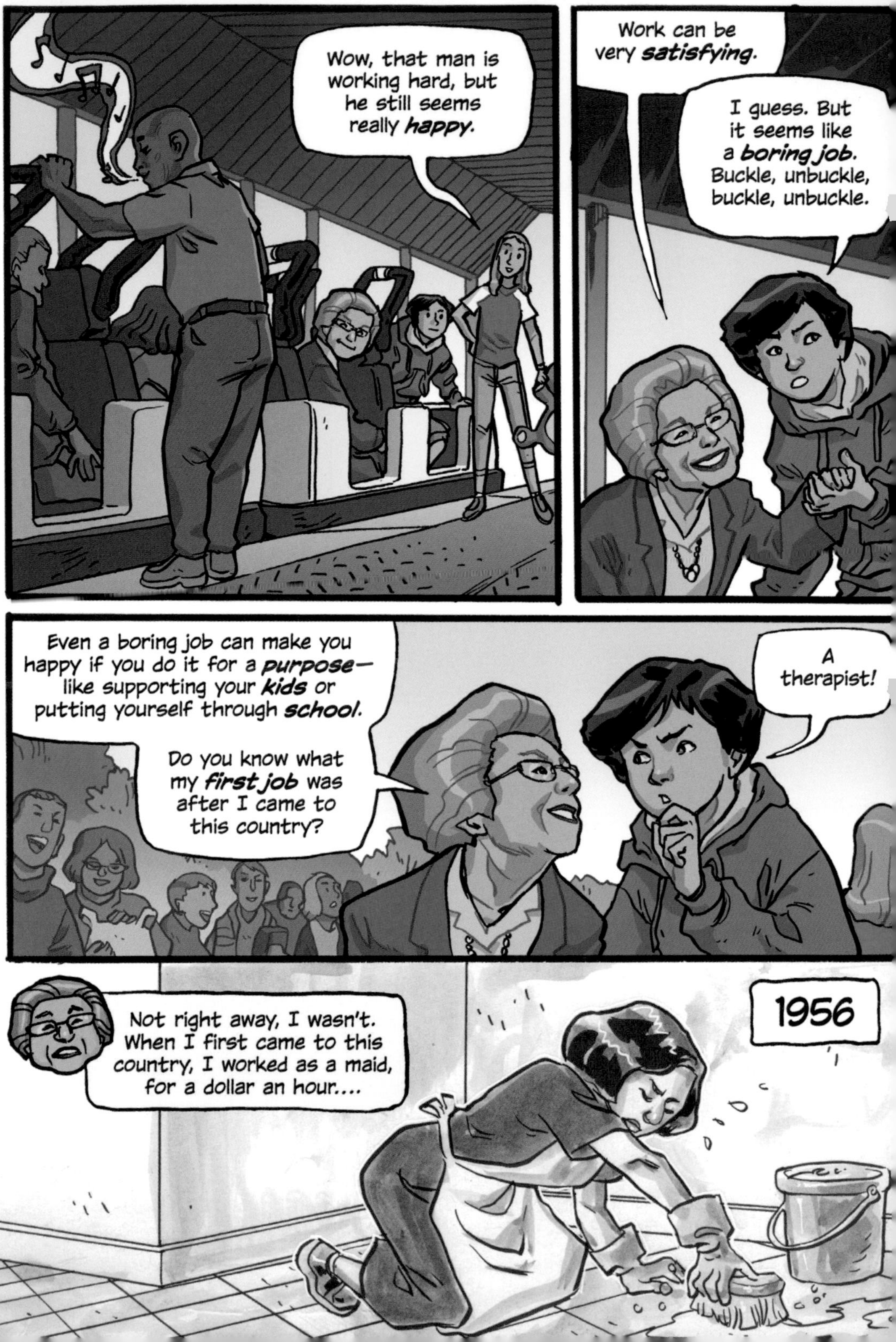
Wow, that man is working hard, but he still seems really happy.
Work can be very satisfying.
I guess. But it seems like a boring job. Buckle, unbuckle, buckle, unbuckle.
Even a boring job can make you happy if you do it for a purpose—like supporting your kids or putting yourself through school.
Do you know what my first job was after I came to this country?
A therapist!
1956
Not right away, I wasn't. When I first came to this country, I worked as a maid, for a dollar an hour....

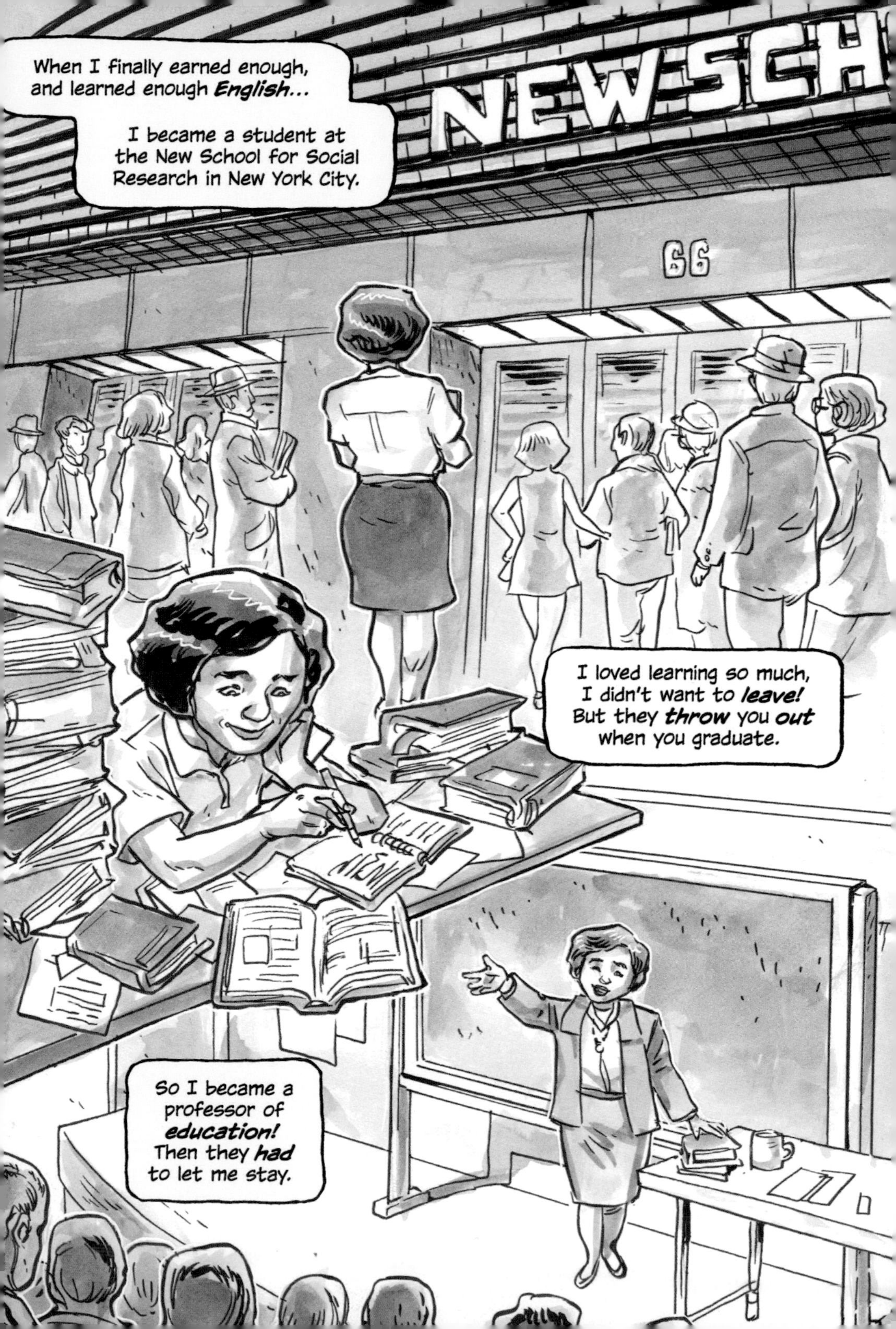

When I finally earned enough, and learned enough **English**...
I became a student at the New School for Social Research in New York City.
NEW SCH
66
I loved learning so much, I didn't want to **leave!** But they **throw** you **out** when you graduate.
So I became a professor of **education!** Then they **had** to let me stay.

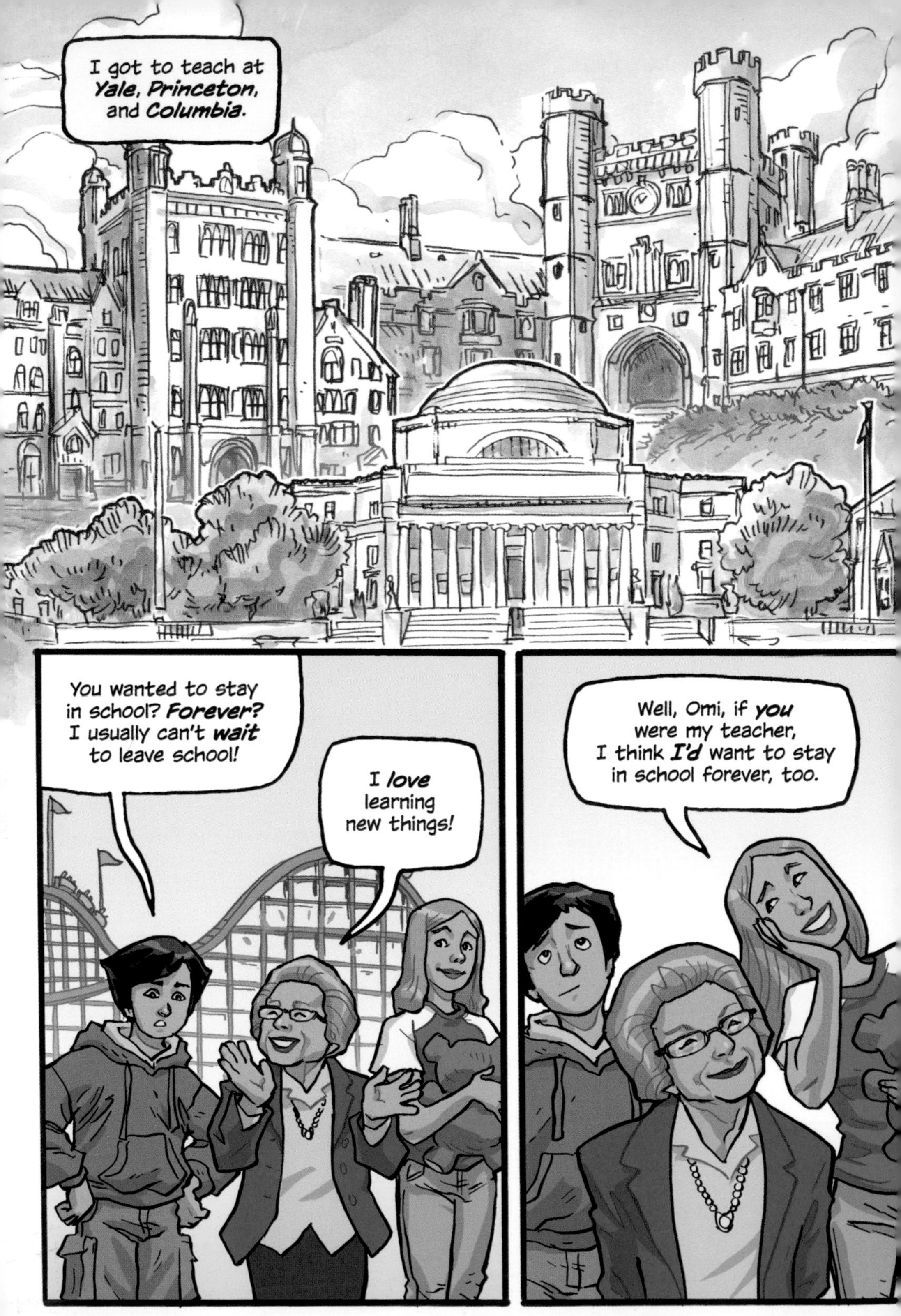
I got to teach at *Yale*, *Princeton*, and *Columbia*.
You wanted to stay in school? *Forever?* I usually can't *wait* to leave school!
I *love* learning new things!
Well, Omi, if *you* were my teacher, I think *I'd* want to stay in school forever, too.

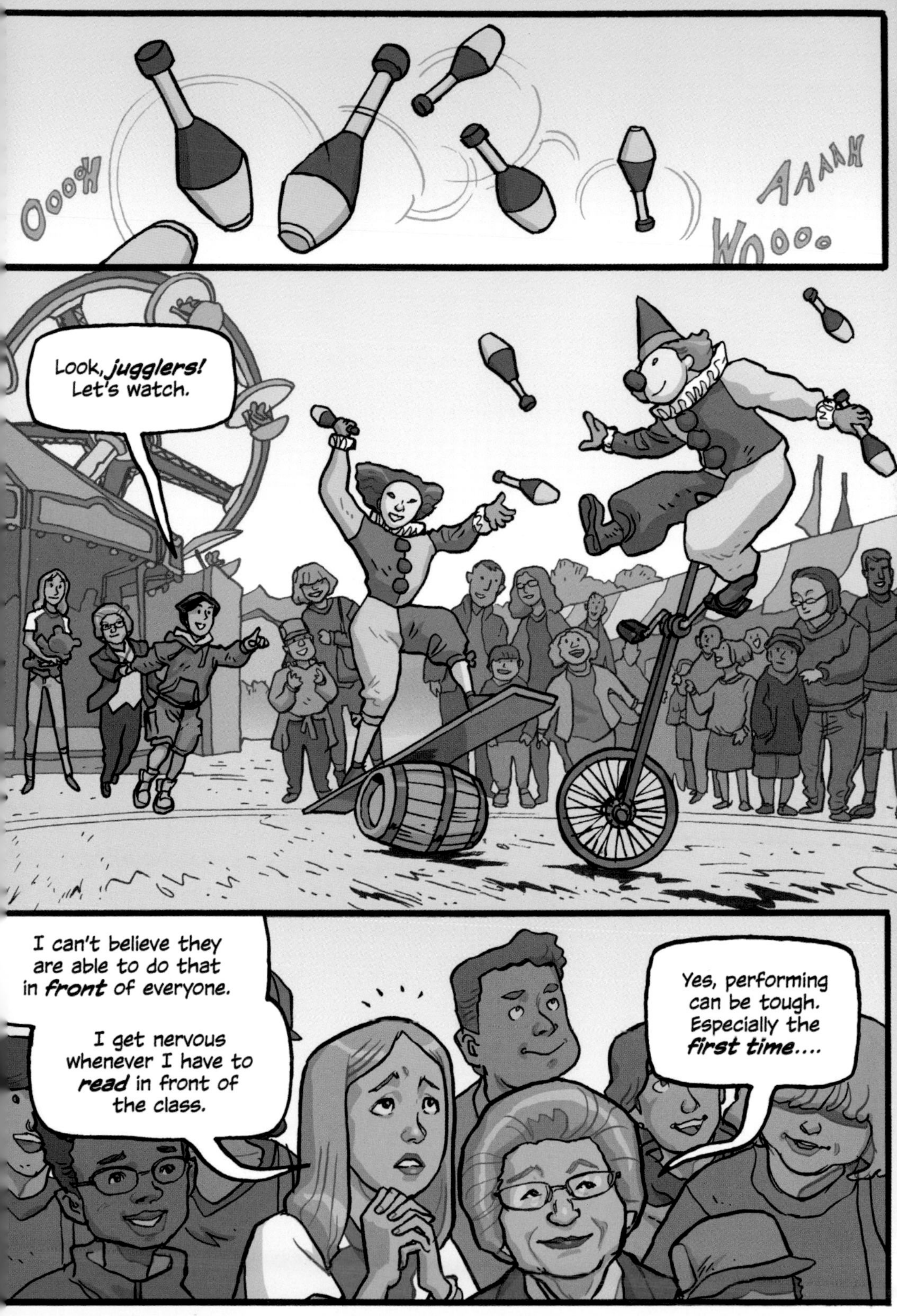
OOOOH
AAAAH
WOOOo
Look, *jugglers!* Let's watch.
I can't believe they are able to do that in *front* of everyone.
I get nervous whenever I have to *read* in front of the class.
Yes, performing can be tough. Especially the *first time*....

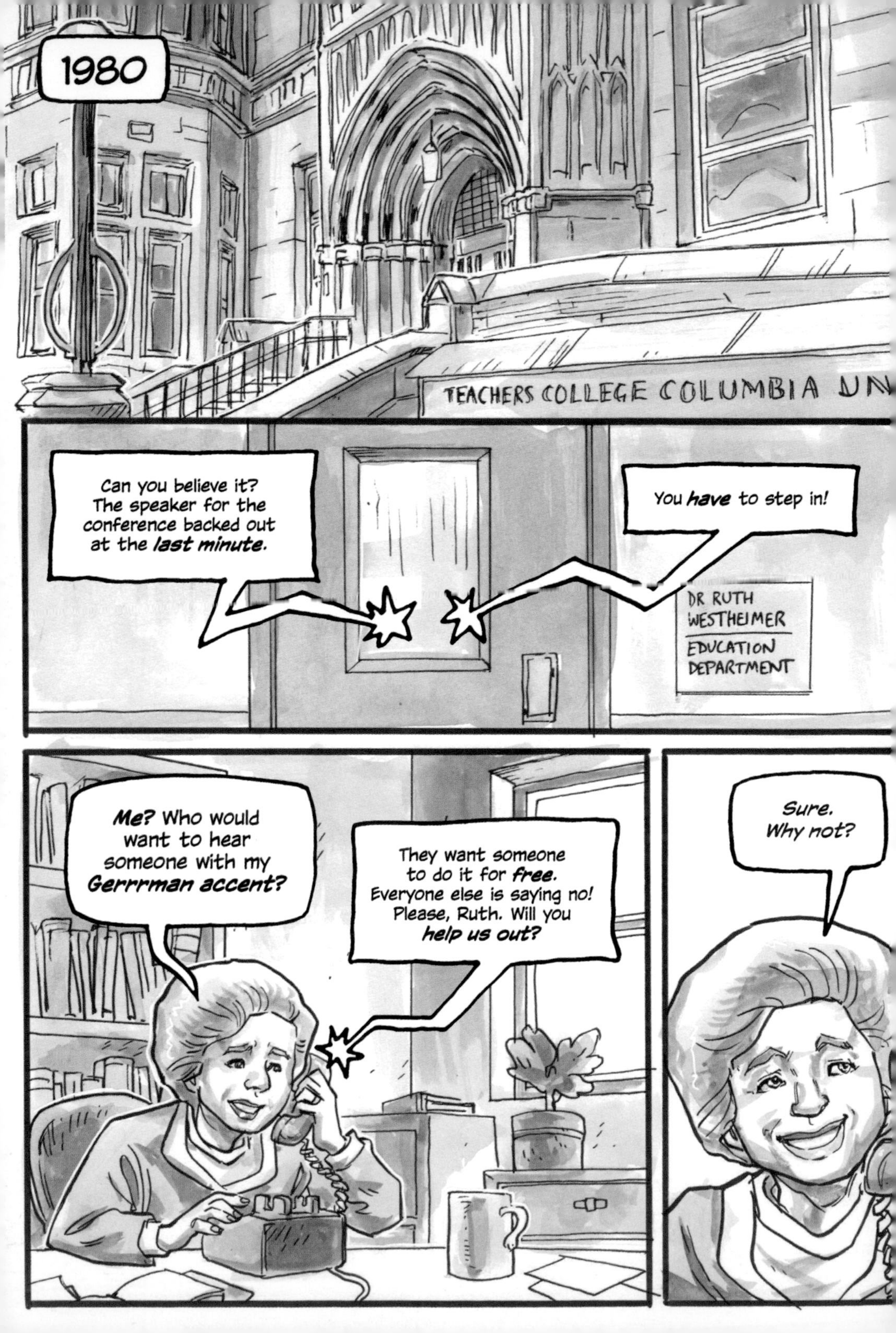
1980
TEACHERS COLLEGE COLUMBIA UN
Can you believe it? The speaker for the conference backed out at the *last minute*.
You *have* to step in!
DR RUTH WESTHEIMER
EDUCATION DEPARTMENT
Me? Who would want to hear someone with my *Gerrrman accent?*
They want someone to do it for *free*. Everyone else is saying no! Please, Ruth. Will you *help us out?*
Sure. Why not?

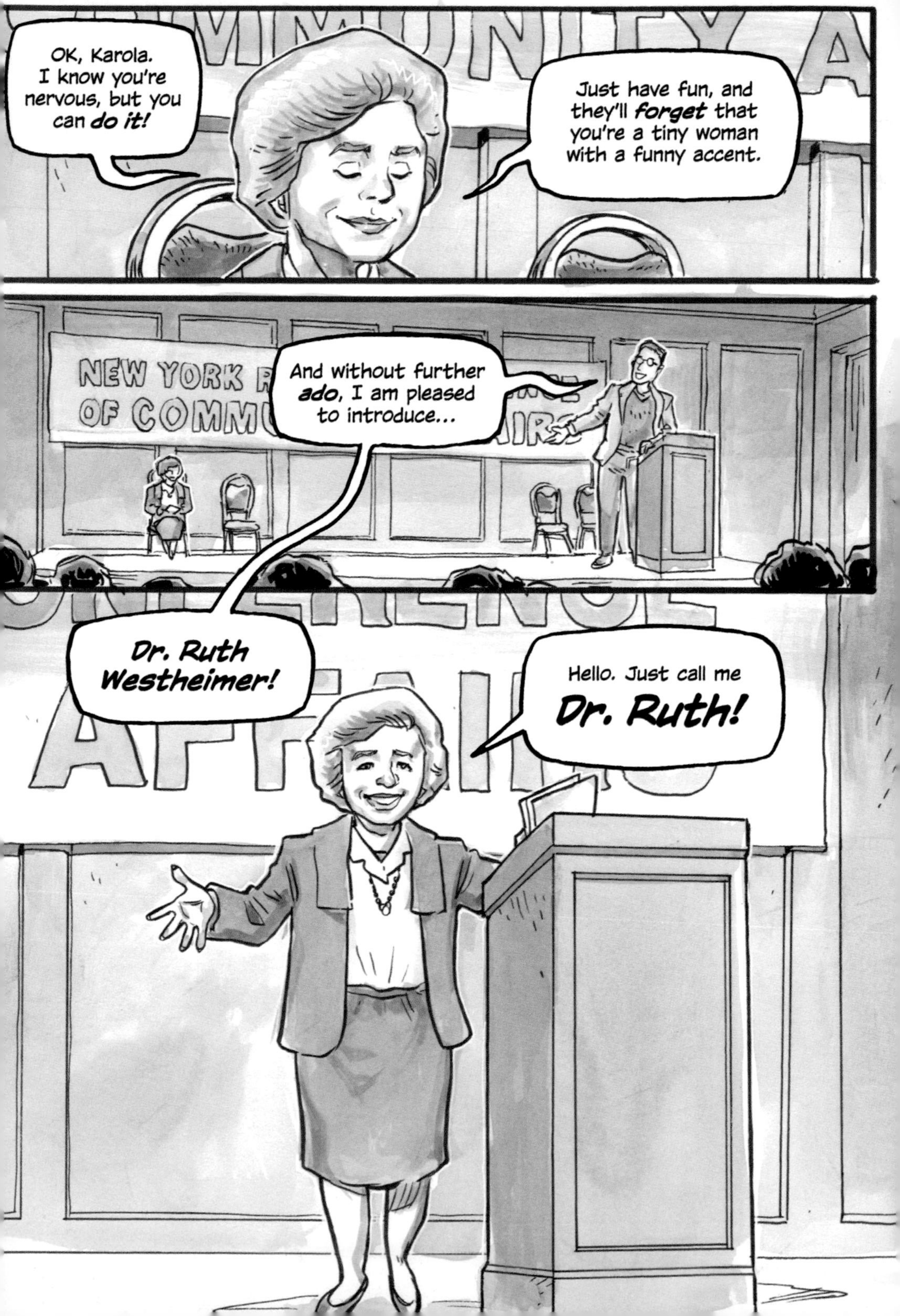
OK, Karola. I know you're nervous, but you can **do it!**
Just have fun, and they'll **forget** that you're a tiny woman with a funny accent.
And without further **ado**, I am pleased to introduce...
Dr. Ruth Westheimer!
Hello. Just call me **Dr. Ruth!**

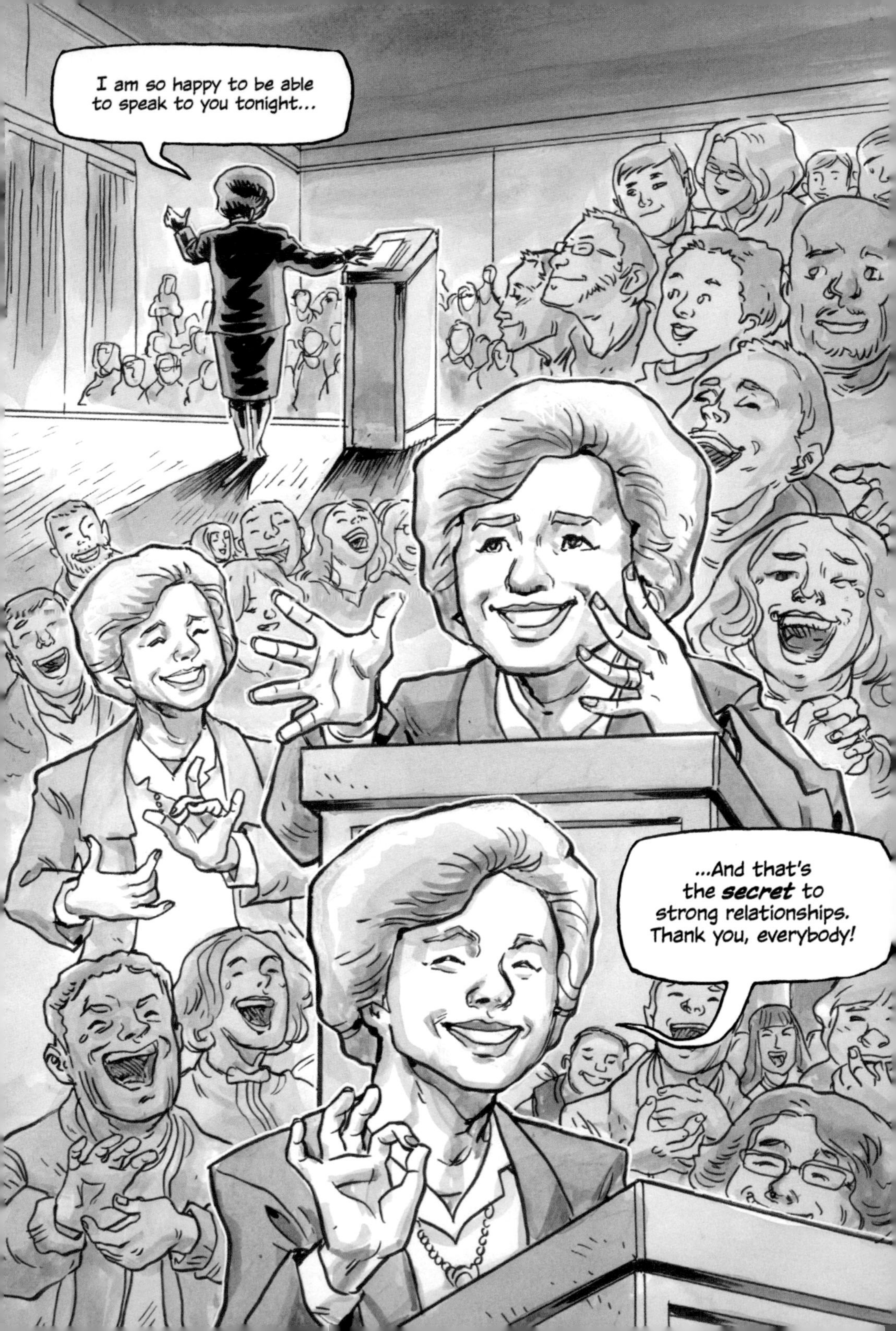
I am so happy to be able to speak to you tonight...
...And that's the *secret* to strong relationships. Thank you, everybody!

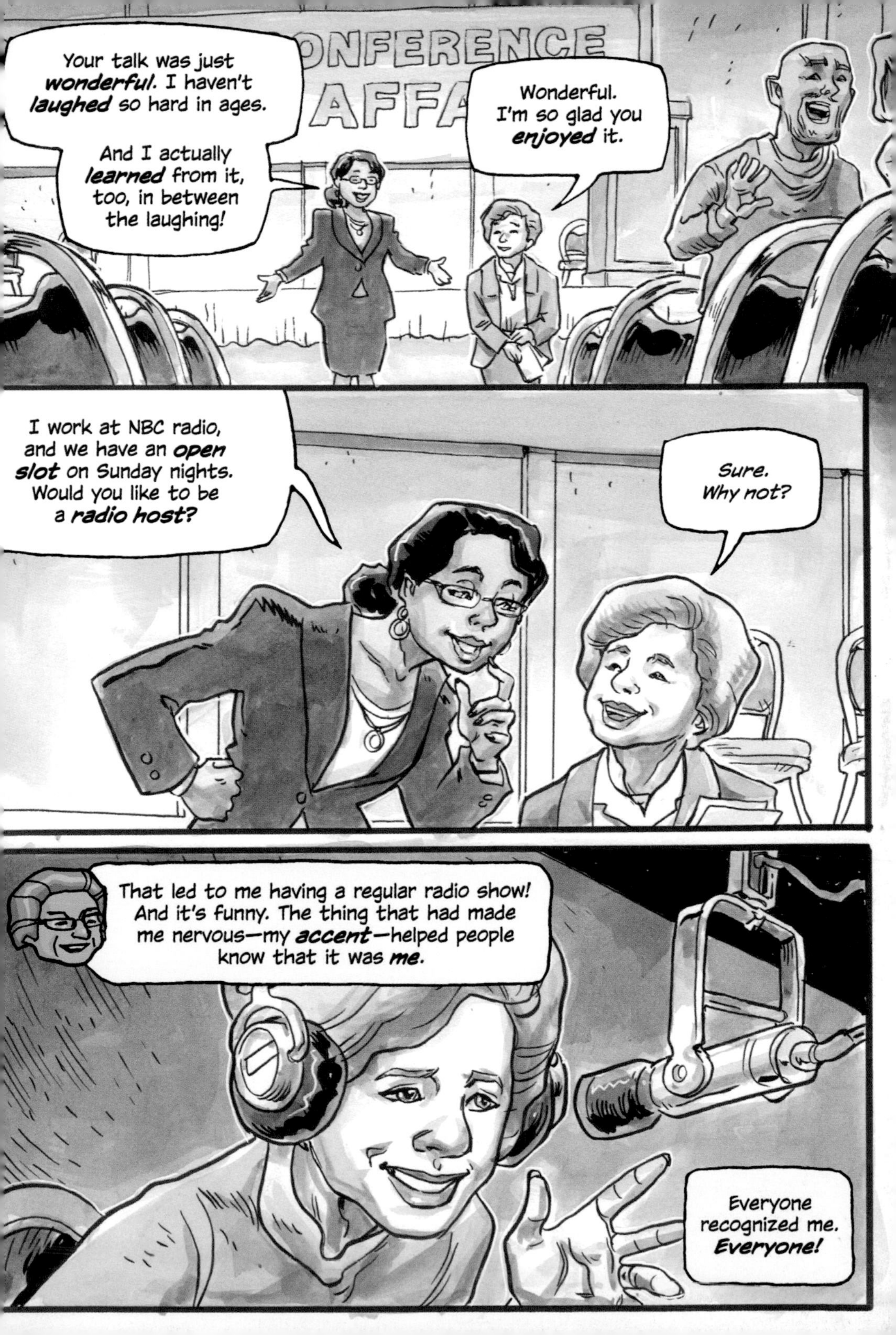

ONFERENCE
AFFA
Your talk was just wonderful. I haven't laughed so hard in ages.
And I actually learned from it, too, in between the laughing!
Wonderful. I'm so glad you enjoyed it.
I work at NBC radio, and we have an open slot on Sunday nights. Would you like to be a radio host?
Sure. Why not?
That led to me having a regular radio show! And it's funny. The thing that had made me nervous—my accent—helped people know that it was me.
Everyone recognized me. Everyone!

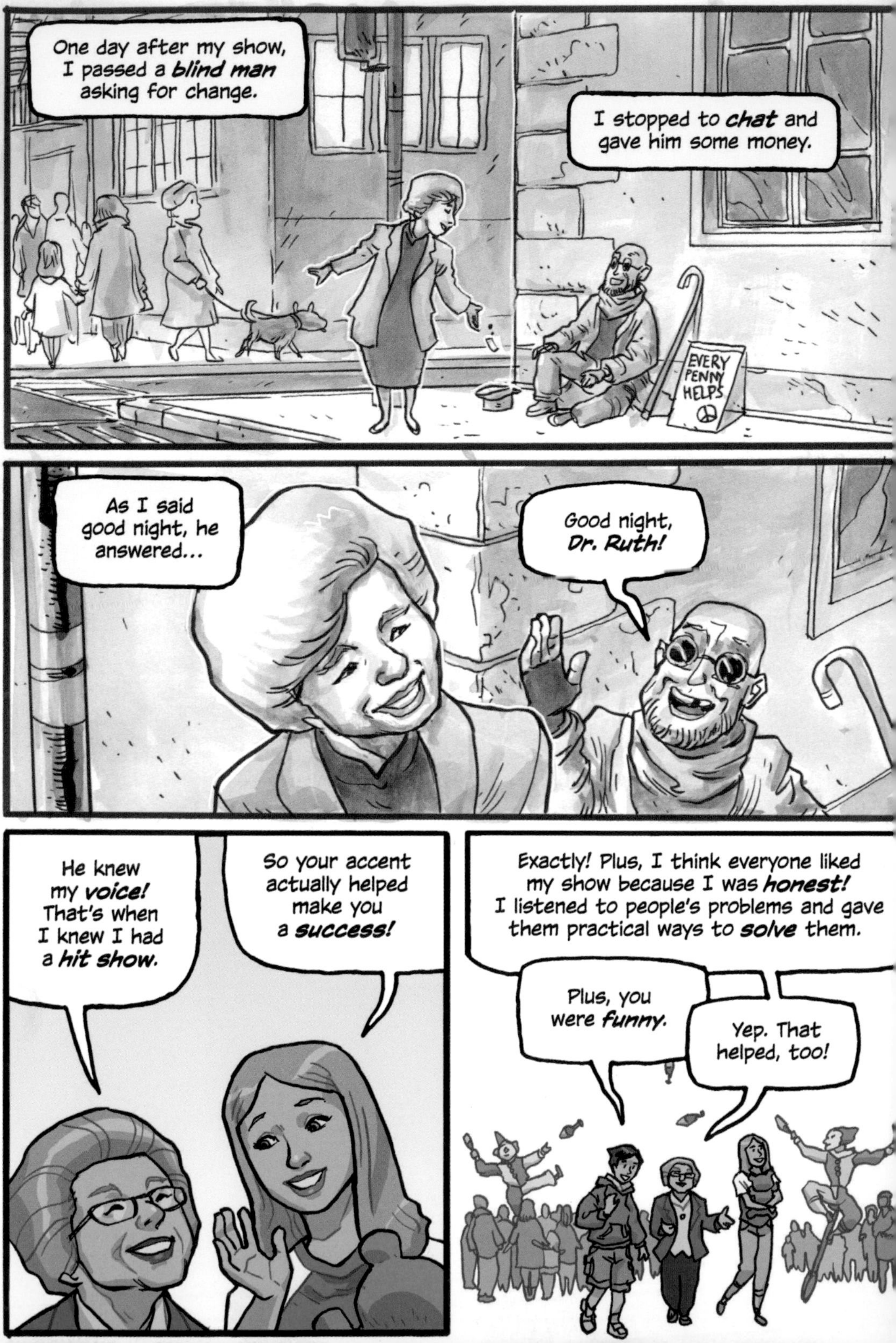

One day after my show, I passed a blind man asking for change.
I stopped to chat and gave him some money.
EVERY PENNY HELPS
As I said good night, he answered...
Good night, Dr. Ruth!
He knew my voice! That's when I knew I had a hit show.
So your accent actually helped make you a success!
Exactly! Plus, I think everyone liked my show because I was honest! I listened to people's problems and gave them practical ways to solve them.
Plus, you were funny.
Yep. That helped, too!

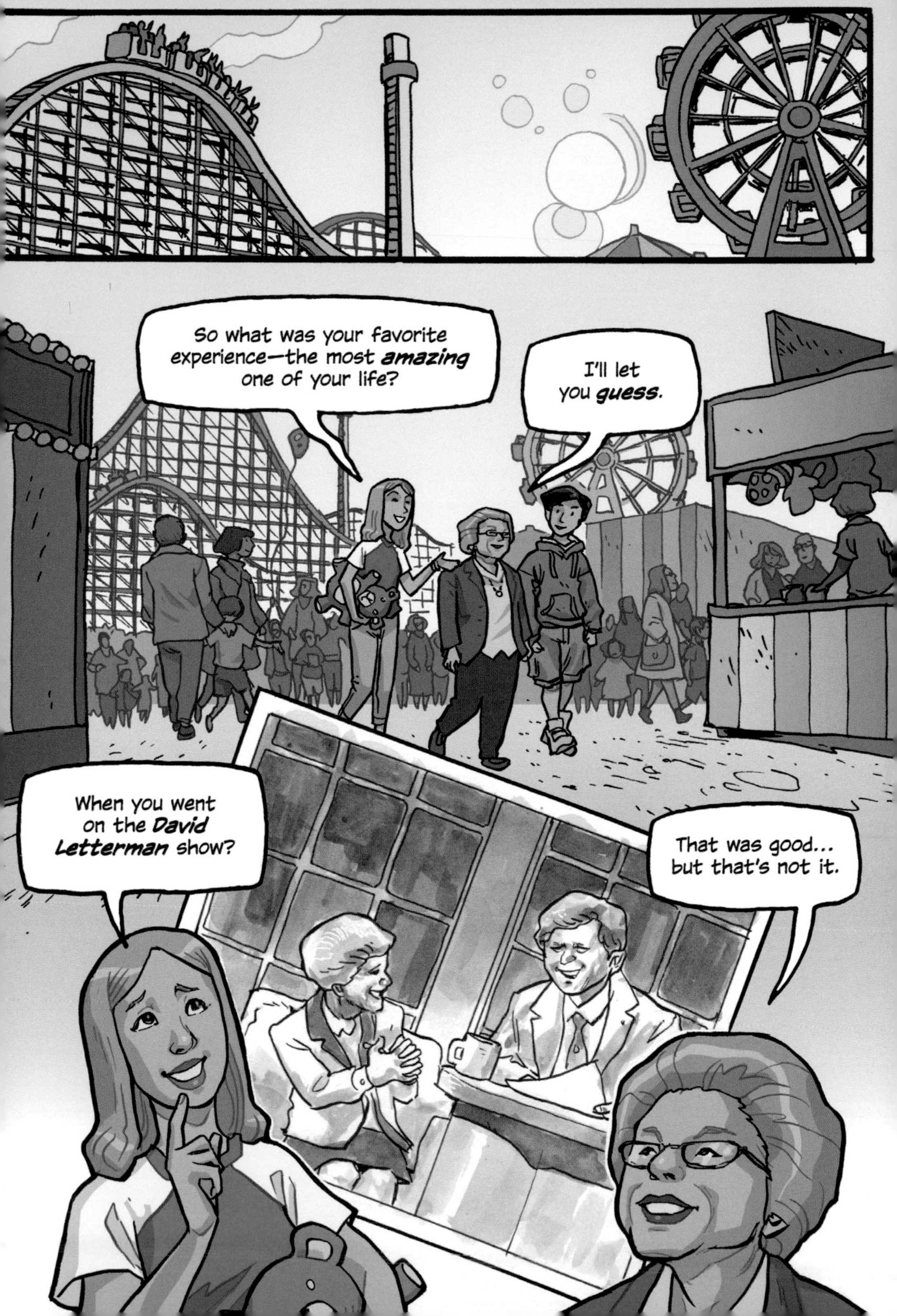
So what was your favorite experience—the most *amazing* one of your life?
I'll let you *guess*.
When you went on the *David Letterman* show?
That was good... but that's not it.

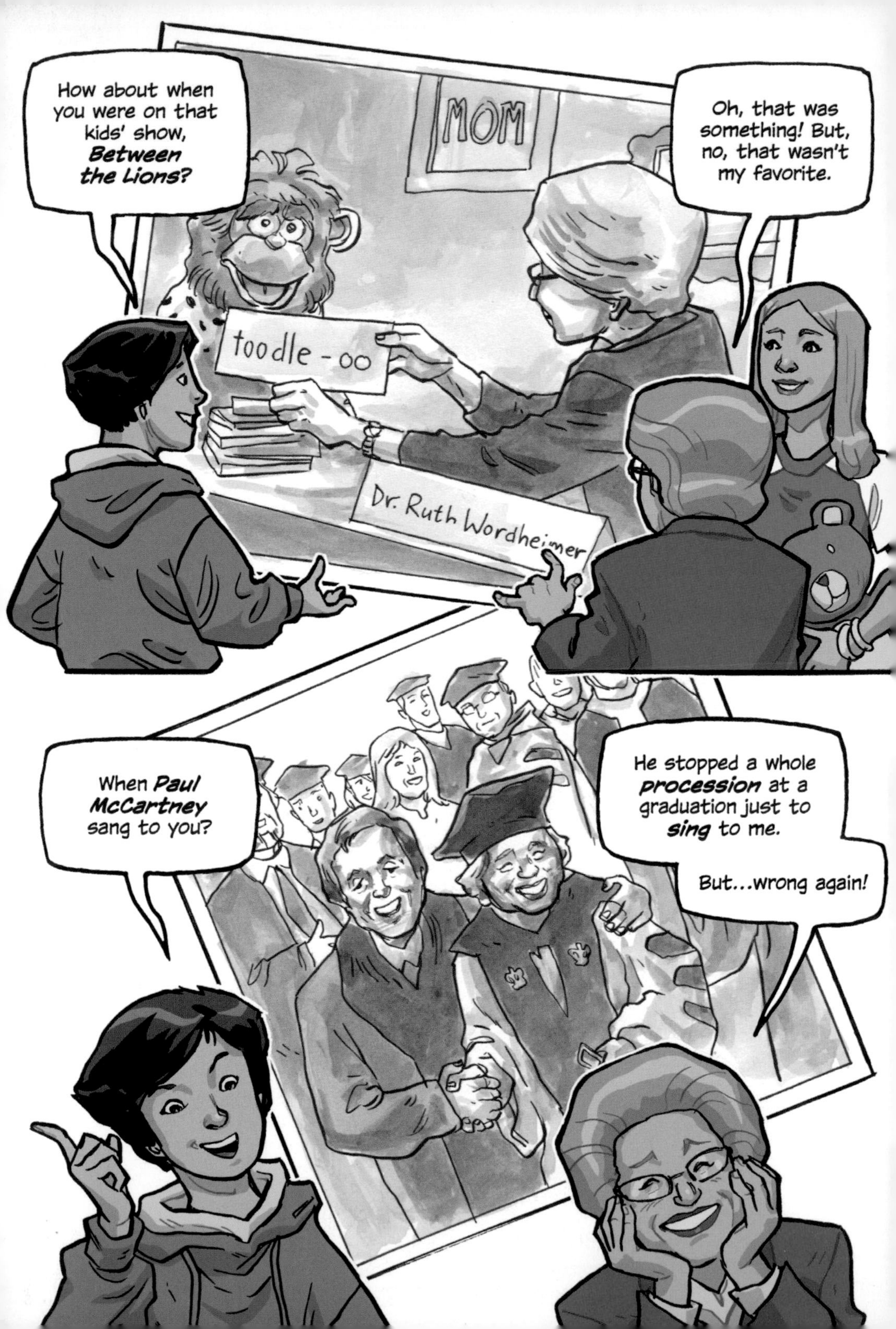
How about when you were on that kids' show, ***Between the Lions?***
MOM
toodle-oo
Dr. Ruth Wordheimer
Oh, that was something! But, no, that wasn't my favorite.
When ***Paul McCartney*** sang to you?
He stopped a whole ***procession*** at a graduation just to ***sing*** to me.
But...wrong again!

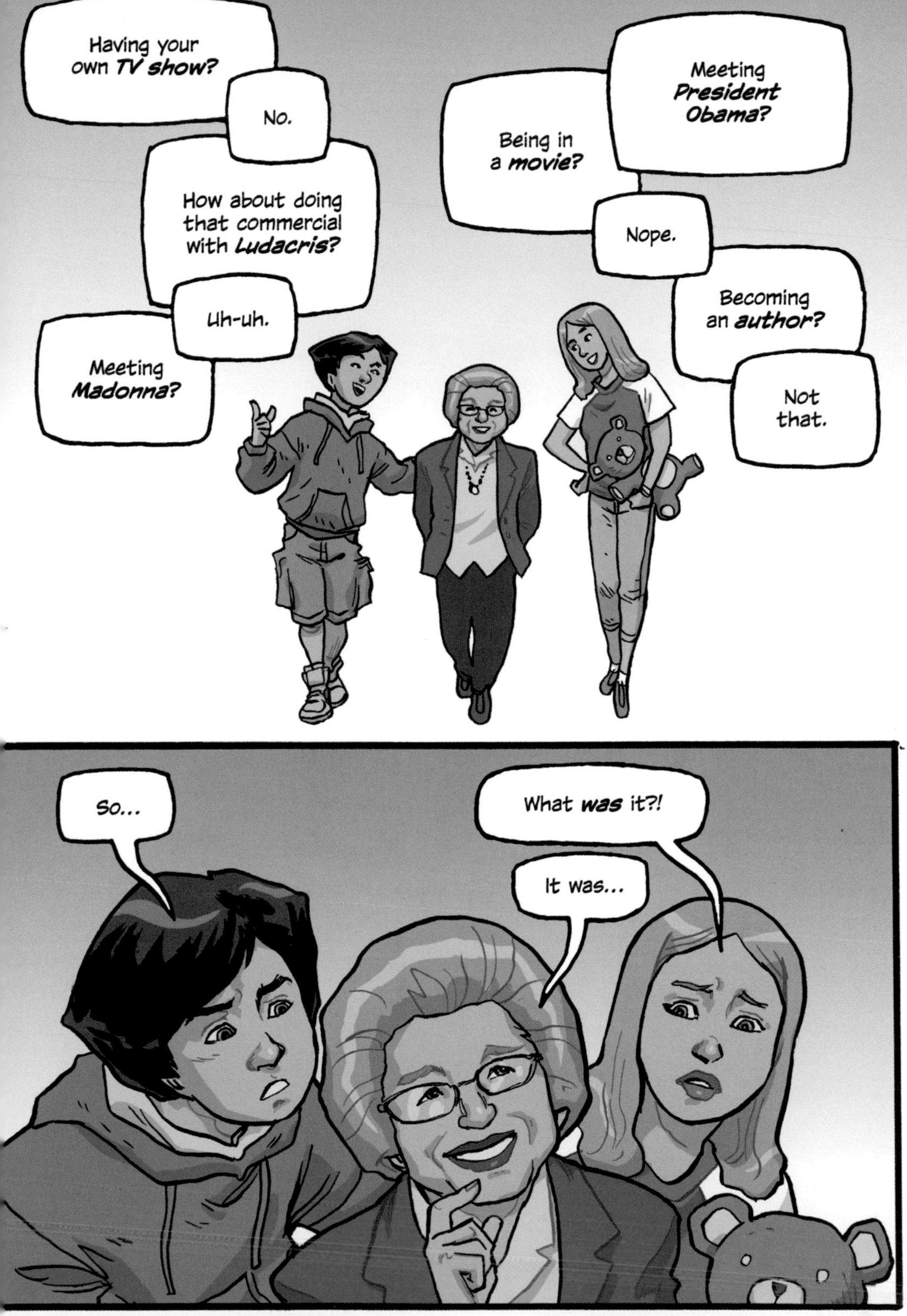
Having your own *TV show?*
No.
How about doing that commercial with *Ludacris?*
Uh-uh.
Meeting *Madonna?*
Being in a *movie?*
Meeting *President Obama?*
Nope.
Becoming an *author?*
Not that.
So...
What *was* it?!
It was...

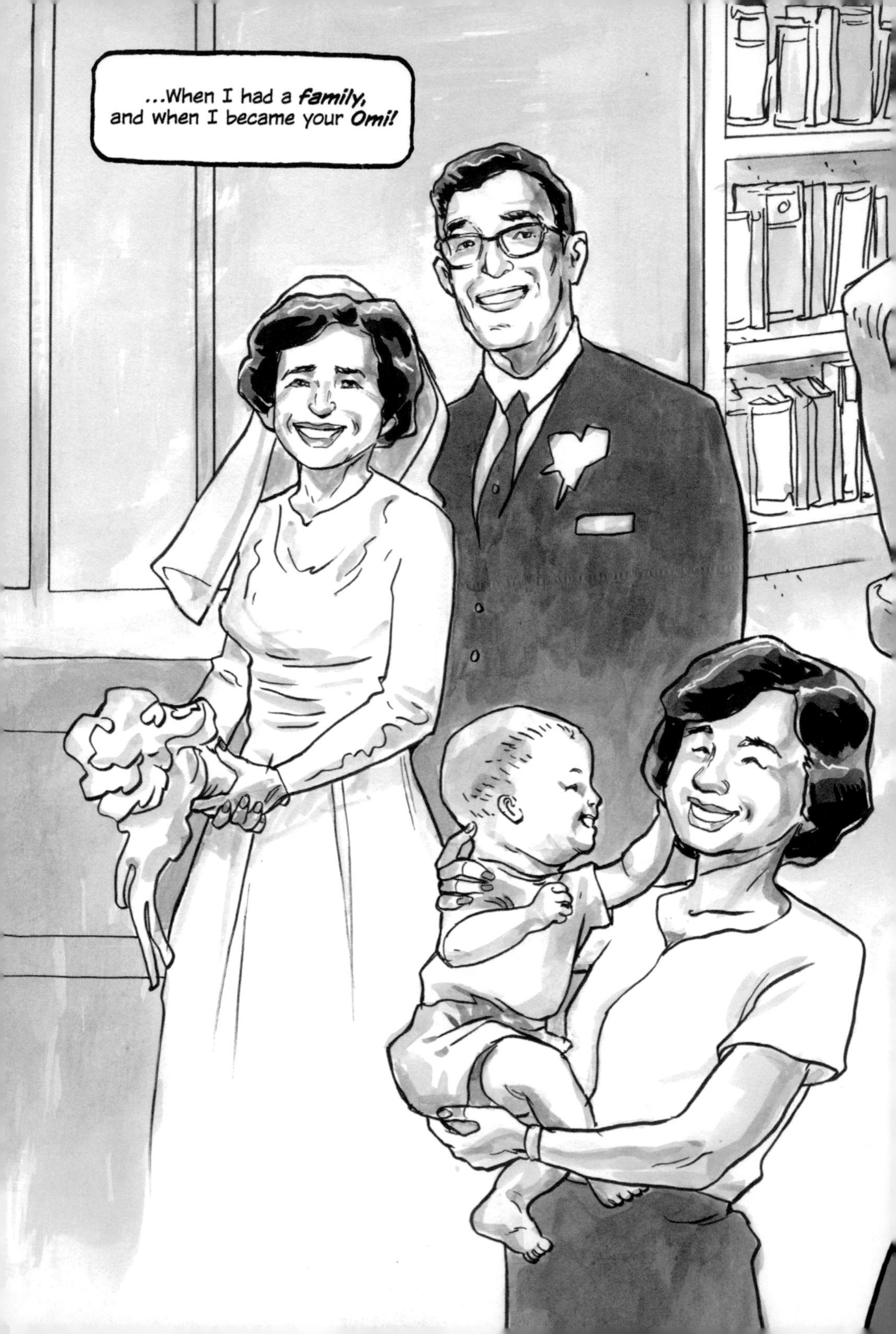
...When I had a *family,* and when I became your *Omi!*

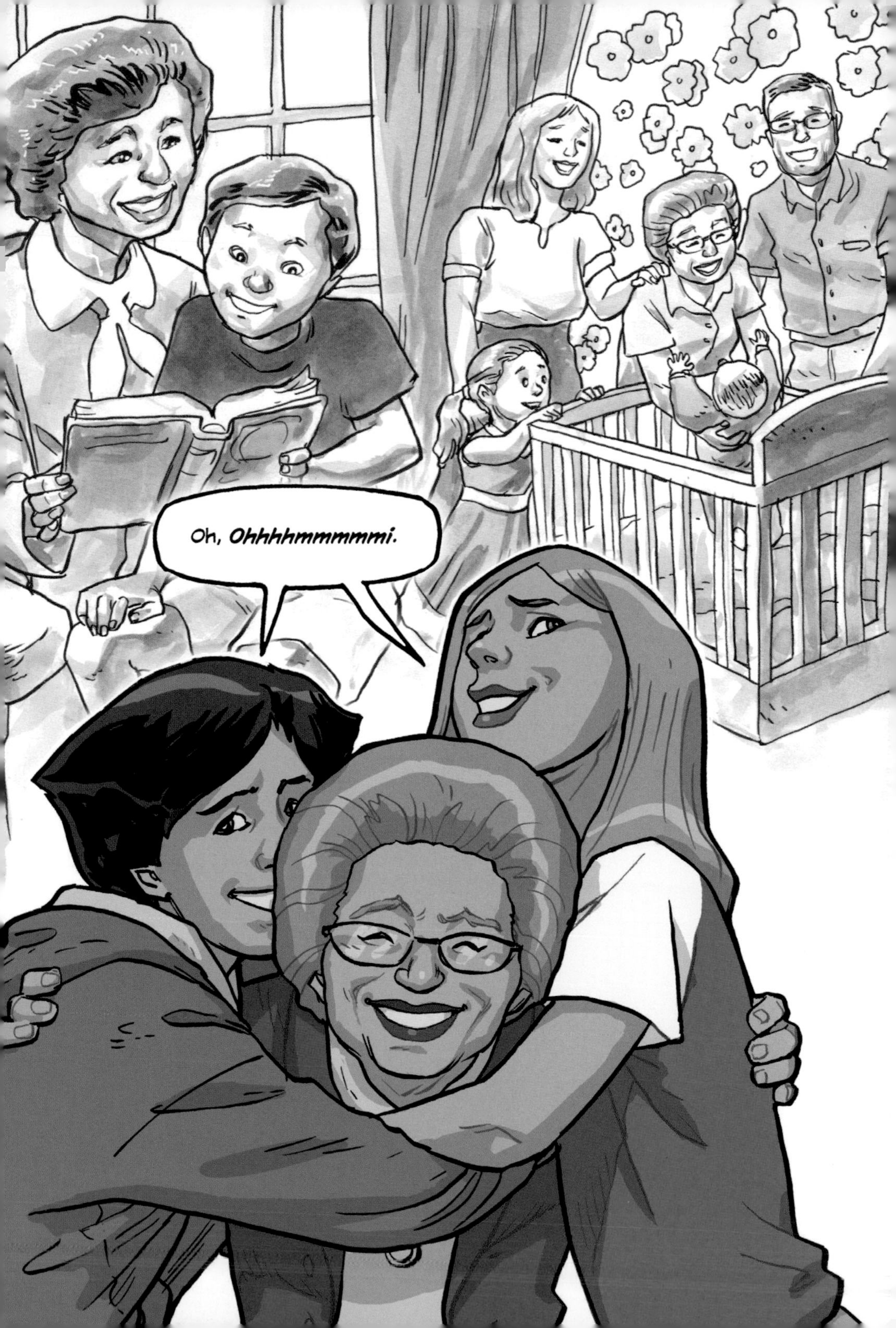
Oh, ***Ohhhhmmmmmi.***

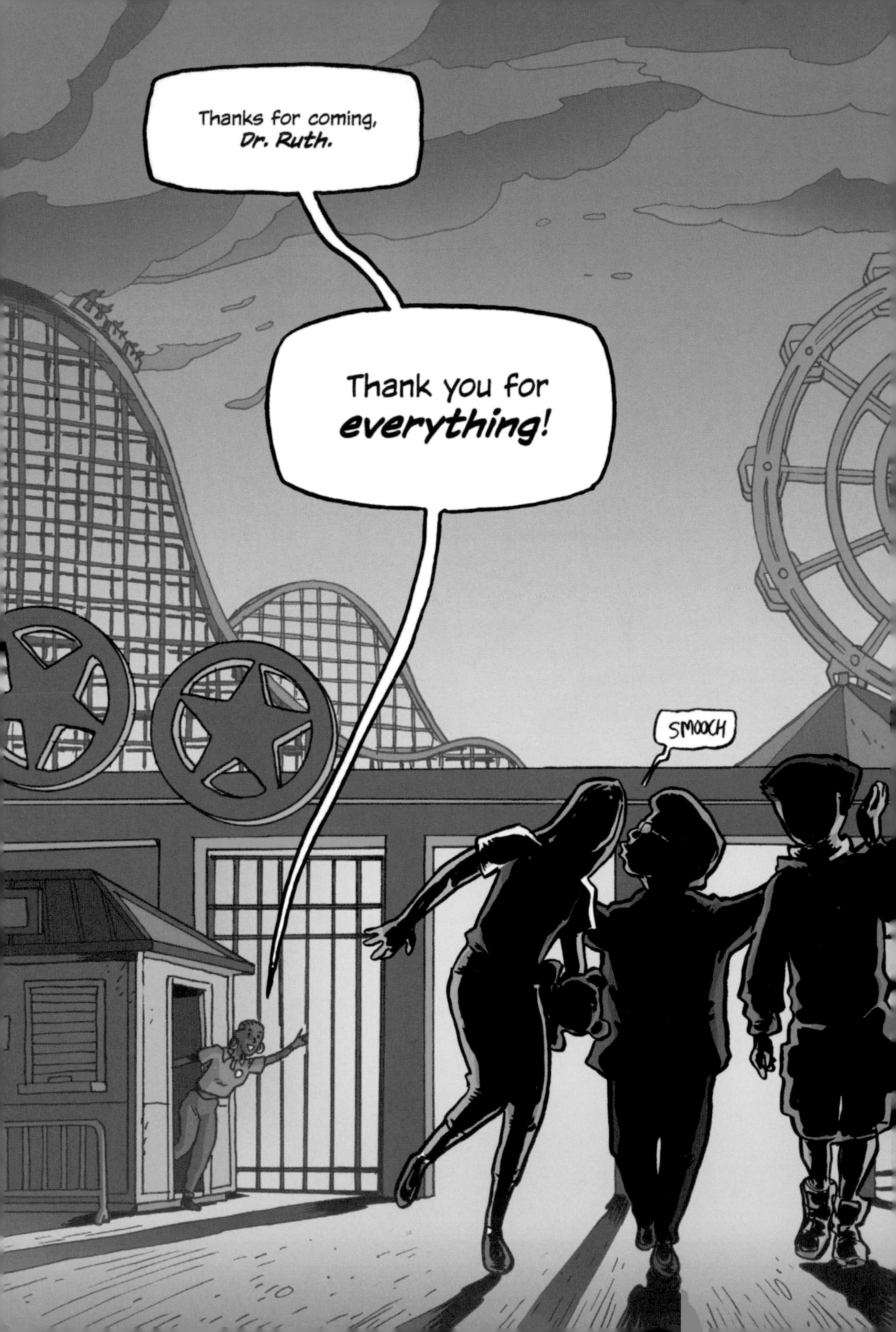
Thanks for coming, *Dr. Ruth.*
Thank you for ***everything***!
SMOOCH

TIMELINE

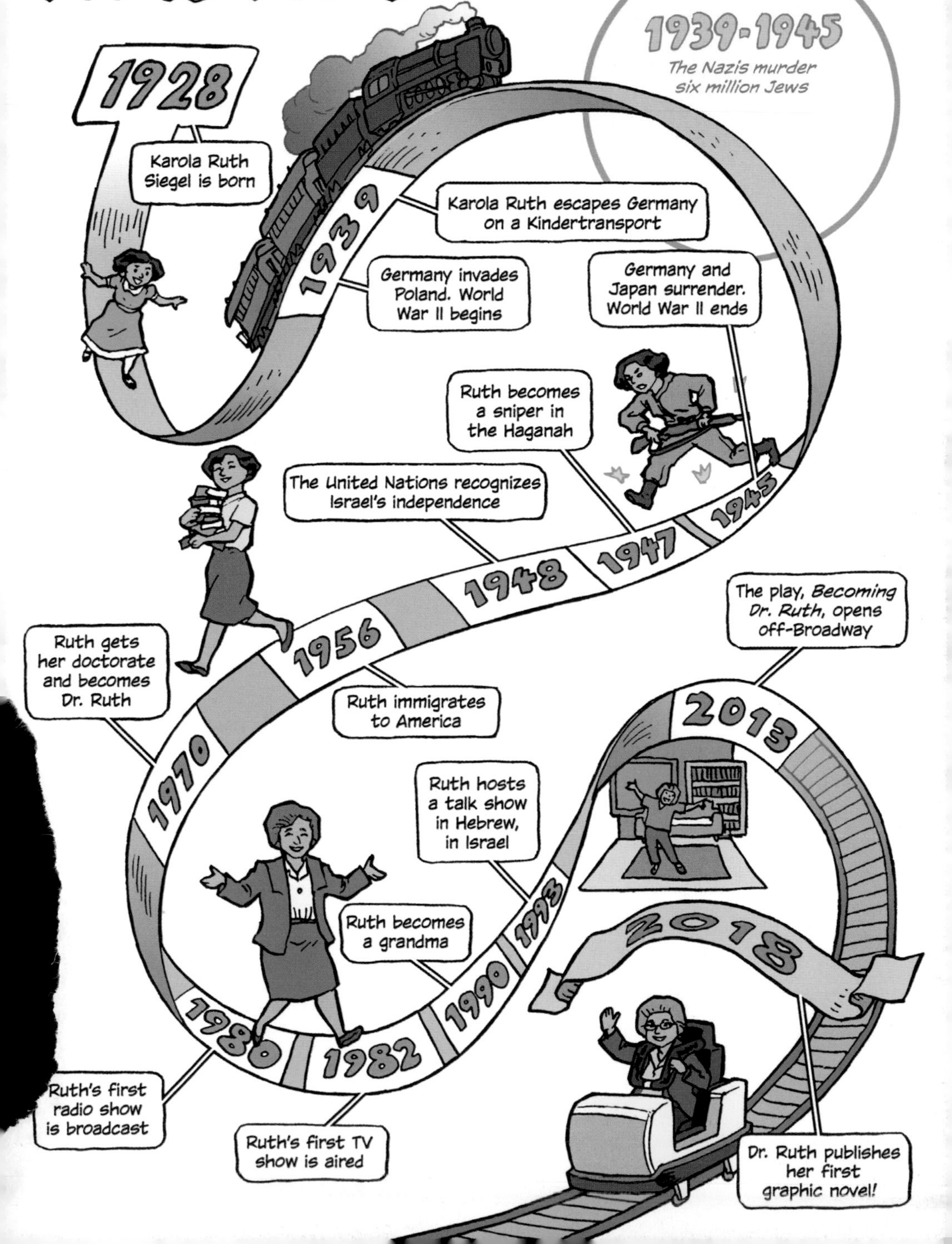
1939-1945
The Nazis murder six million Jews
1928
Karola Ruth Siegel is born
1939
Karola Ruth escapes Germany on a Kindertransport
Germany invades Poland. World War II begins
1945
Germany and Japan surrender. World War II ends
1947
Ruth becomes a sniper in the Haganah
1948
The United Nations recognizes Israel's independence
1956
Ruth immigrates to America
1970
Ruth gets her doctorate and becomes Dr. Ruth
1980
Ruth's first radio show is broadcast
1982
Ruth's first TV show is aired
1990
Ruth becomes a grandma
1993
Ruth hosts a talk show in Hebrew, in Israel
2013
The play, *Becoming Dr. Ruth*, opens off-Broadway
2018
Dr. Ruth publishes her first graphic novel!

RUTH'S LIFE HAS BEEN A WILD RIDE

Karola Ruth Siegel, age ten, 1938

BUT WHAT DOES HER STORY MEAN TO YOU?

✔ How does Ruth's story make you think differently about your own life?

✔ Which qualities of Ruth's personality do you want to make part of your life? How can you apply those qualities to face challenges in your life?

✔ Ruth gives lots of advice to her grandkids! What parts of her advice do you want to apply to your life, and how?

Dr. Ruth K. Westheimer is a therapist and educator whose humorous and open style has made her wildly popular across the globe. She has entertained and inspired millions of fans through her radio and television shows, as well as through her books and articles. Dr. Westheimer, a widow, has two children and four grandchildren. She lives in New York City.

Dr. Ruth K. Westheimer at age eighty

Pierre A. Lehu Pierre A. Lehu is a publicist, agent, and writer. He has written twenty-nine books, including *Saké: Water from Heaven*, *Fashion for Dummies*, and *Living on Your Own*.

Mark Simmons is a 2009 graduate of the Academy of Art University. His specialties include comics, storyboards, sequential art, and giant robots. His work can be seen at www.ultimatemark.com.